D1462025

SPECIAL MESSAGE TO READERS
THE ULVERSCROFT FOUNDATION
(registered UK charity number 264873)
was established in 1972 to provide funds for research, diagnosis and treatment of eye diseases. Examples of major projects funded by the Ulverscroft Foundation are:

- The Children's Eye Unit at Moorfields Eye Hospital, London
- The Ulverscroft Children's Eye Unit at Great Ormond Street Hospital for Sick Children
- Funding research into eye diseases and treatment at the Department of Ophthalmology, University of Leicester
- The Ulverscroft Vision Research Group, Institute of Child Health
- Twin operating theatres at the Western Ophthalmic Hospital, London
- The Chair of Ophthalmology at the Royal Australian College of Ophthalmologists

You can help further the work of the Foundation by making a donation or leaving a legacy. Every contribution is gratefully received. If you would like to help support the Foundation or require further information, please contact:

THE ULVERSCROFT FOUNDATION
The Green, Bradgate Road, Anstey
Leicester LE7 7FU, England
Tel: (0116) 236 4325
website: www.ulverscroft-foundation.org.uk

ESTHER, BABY

Esther Chambers appears to have it all. As the beautiful star model at hip 1960s boutique Attitude, she captures the affections of charismatic private investigator Jude Dunbar. However, she has jealous enemies, and the traumatic secrets of both her recent past and long ago are about to spill out. Can she and Jude save her kidnapped friend, foil the baddies, and solve the mystery of who Esther actually is?

DEBBIE CHASE

ESTHER, BABY

Complete and Unabridged

LINFORD
Leicester

First published in Great Britain in 2021

First Linford Edition
published 2022

A catalogue record for this book is available from the British Library.

ISBN 978–1–4448–4919–6

Published by
Ulverscroft Limited
Anstey, Leicestershire

Printed and bound in Great Britain by
TJ Books Ltd., Padstow, Cornwall

This book is printed on acid-free paper

1

London, 1965

Martha Engleson, dresses, coats and skirts hung over her arm like the drooping neck of a swan, swished open the blood-red changing room curtains before saying, 'Hey Esther baby, some guy's just come in with a woman looks old enough to be his mother. She wants to see these pronto.'

Reluctantly I stood up, carefully putting a bookmark into my book *In Cold Blood* by Truman Capote — a new release just begging to be read, or so the reviews had said. I'd been flicking through the pages waiting for my turn for the shop floor. Jane, Julie and Pam were already out there strutting their stuff.

Martha hung the clothes on a rack and pointed backwards with her thumb like a hitchhiker, shaking her head.

'She's gotta be his mother — but him,

Esther baby — wow.' And then without stopping for a breath while peering over my shoulder, she continued, 'What ya reading? Hey, I've heard about that book, true story and all . . . wiped out a whole family. Some people, huh?'

I yawned and stretched, stiff after having been sitting for so long.

'Hmm, I'm not sure if I'm gonna read it all through yet . . .'

'Yeah well, put the book down and get yourself motivated. This couple, they asked for you, the one who looks like Grace Kelly, they said . . . you know how popular you are, Esther baby. You shouldn't be working as a model in one of London's top stores if you wanna sit around and read all day.'

Yeah, OK, I knew that was true. Attitude boutique on Carnaby Street was definitely the place to go in swinging London for the best clothes, that was for sure. My workplace was on a par with other up and coming boutiques like Roxette and London Girl, and even Carnaby Clothing.

It was by no means cheap, yet in Attitude you could buy good items, affordable quality. The clothes were quirky, too, ranging from maxi to midi to mini, from jeans to woollen leggings, and from flip flops and gladiator sandals to go-go boots. The choice was amazing.

All the best, most sought-after models worked here — not just for the chance to wear unusual, well made items but the money too. Attitude paid more per hour than the average boutique or department store.

'What's she thinking?' Martha muttered to herself, as she rifled through the clothes with stubby fingers. 'None of these will fit her, she's the size of a house! And I'm talking a big house here, a mansion, not a 1930s semi.' And then louder, to me, 'Not like you, Esther baby, all tall and willowy, and your beauty . . . well!'

Martha had come here all the way from New York. Hence the 'Esther baby,' which I hadn't minded at first but now everyone, even the other models, were calling me it.

How would they like it? *Hey Jane baby*, *Julie baby*, *Pam baby*, you get what I mean? There'd been a Jo baby, but she'd been taken away by the police only last week for modelling exotic lingerie in the shop window.

Oh yeah, live models were quite the thing nowadays and London was a really exciting place to be.

'Yes, well,' I replied, touching the silkiness of a dress, and the weightiness of a skirt, sparkles hand-stitched laboriously around the hem, before ducking behind the curtain. I started to take off my own clothes, which slithered to the floor and pooled at my feet like water. 'Beauty is in the eye of the beholder.'

'Yeah, and that's just about every eye of every man that comes in this place.' Martha nodded emphatically, knowing she was right, standing with her hands on her hips, her flowered pinny tight around her ample waist.

While Martha was there to help all the models with clothes changes and upkeep, she tended to stick with me — which didn't exactly help in the Esther popularity stakes, especially with Pam.

Jane and Julie didn't seem to be bothered either way but Pam was definitely not a fan of Esther Chambers, that was for sure. I asked Martha not to make it so obvious that she did more for me than for the other girls, but she said that the others could go hoot as far as she was concerned. Whatever that meant.

I caught a glimpse of myself in the mirror. Esther Chambers, aged twenty-two, blessed with thick ash-blonde hair sometimes put up in a chignon à la Grace Kelly. Large, brown Bette Davis eyes, a pouty pink mouth, high cheekbones, smooth velvety skin and an hourglass figure. Yeah, OK, if beauty was measured in gold I'd be rich! No doubt about that.

'Zip me up, Martha,' I said, as I pulled on the first outfit, a really cool black shift mini-dress worn with white tights and black leather knee-high boots.

'There you go, Esther baby, now go

wow 'em.'

Martha gave me a gentle tap on the back, pushing me forward, as I sashayed out from between the curtains into the shop to stand before our potential customer.

She was, as Martha had said, built like the side of a house, with a face as round as the moon, her cheeks hanging in deep folds like a morose dog — hmm, what's that phrase about a bulldog chewing a wasp? She had a heavy figure with a large bosom that stuck out like a shelf, and was clothed in black, a small hat perched on her head like a pea on a drum.

He was sitting by her side watching me intently as I posed, hands on hips, slowly revolving around like a wheel so they could see the outfit from every angle.

I had an overall impression of good looks and rich clothing and a man maybe three or four years older than me. On peering from beneath my eyelashes, I saw that he had red-gold hair that sprang crisply from his forehead, and a sprinkling of soft stubble covering his upper lip and chin like a young boy's first growth. His blue eyes twinkled like lights — he was a real lookalike for that charismatic actor, Paul Newman. I'd gone to the flicks a couple of years ago to see *The Hustler* and had stared at the screen with wide eyes the whole time. Wow!

I caught a whiff of a sultry perfume and then something masculine and spicy, making me catch my breath — Old Spice perhaps. He wore a tan overcoat and a fedora hat that he swung idly from his middle finger as he concentrated on me, watching with narrowed baby blues as I revolved like a beautiful carousel.

From the corner of my eye I glimpsed Jane and Julie modelling alongside me, other prospective buyers ogling intently. Jane was wearing a dress, long and blue with a high neckline and long transparent sleeves, a massive floppy hat on her head. Julie sported a mini-skirt, a snug fitted polo-necked jumper tucked in to show a thin gold chain belt around her tiny waist, and gladiator sandals that curled around her legs to the thigh like snakes. All three of us wore heavy eye make-up, thick and black, with long, curling false lashes and a slick of pale pink frosted lipstick, rosy brown blusher on our cheeks.

Martha was ready to help at every dress change, not only with her hands but her mouth as well.

'Wow . . . you see him?' The pull up or down of a zip. 'The Paul Newman lookalike?' The straightening of a hem. 'What's he doing with her?' A vicious pull to expose more bosom. 'So, is she his mother, you think?' The teasing of a pair of gloves over outstretched fingers. 'He likes you, Esther baby. I see the way he looks at you . . . oh yeah.'

'You say that of every man that comes in here,' I hissed, taking once more to the catwalk, clad this time in a maxi emerald-green gown, sporting a huge decorative bow at the waist and set off by long white gloves to the elbow. I saw the bulldog woman nudge 'Paul Newman' and nod her head as he made a note on a pad with a silver pen.

* * *

Several nudges and notes later and I was done for the day, changing out of the last outfit and shrugging on a loose robe, tying it tight at the waist, before sitting at the mirror to remove my heavy make-up with cleanser and cotton wool. Martha was nattering at my elbow as she checked out the clothes for any tears or marks before hanging them back on the rail and then, after looking at her watch, announcing that she was going home now.

Jane, Julie and Pam — she of long red hair and cat-green eyes — smoked as they wiped their faces, cigarettes hanging from the corners of their mouths or between yellow-tipped fingers and smoke swirling above our heads. I couldn't abide the dirty habit and coughed loud and long despite getting enough snide glances to make myself unpopular for years to come. Although I was already that anyway, because of Martha.

'See you tomorrow, girls,' I said as I finished getting dressed and prepared to leave the changing rooms. I'd already checked my locker but it was empty and as I barely used it, left it open, the key dangling from the lock.

They all gave little wiggly waves, Pam taking an extra-long drag on her cigarette and belching out the smoke like a chimney stack in my direction.

'Good night, Esther baby,' she said sarcastically.

'Have a good evening,' I replied totally unperturbed, as I closed the door softly behind me.

'Who does she think she is?' I heard Pam say as I loitered at the door. 'Just cos she's more than average pretty . . .'

'Got a pretty bad cough though, hasn't she?' Jane smirked.

'Hey, come on,' protested Julie. 'Esther's OK . . . just a really proud person, that's all.'

Totally ignoring that comment, Pam said, 'What's that saying? If you don't like the smoke get out of the changing room?' They all laughed, loud and tinkling as bells ringing, and then Pam added, 'Somebody needs to teach her a lesson!'

I didn't care what they said, despite my racing heart. I had to think of myself first. They were just there, background people, always judging me on my appearance, always making digs about my looks and wondering why, just because I was pretty, that I was timid and had no backbone and would be scared of a few choice words flung in my direction. I could stick up for myself, but I chose not to this time.

I clattered down the steep stone steps leading to the back door of the building, the staff door, slingbacks barely on and legs clad in skin tone stockings, cream trench coat belted tight, my leather bag slung over one shoulder. I flung a scarf over my hair and tied it under my chin as I squeezed through the door and out into the cold, dank air.

A security light flared bright white, even though it wasn't quite dark yet, showing a creepy cobbled lane to the side of the building dotted with big silver bins and piles of rubbish. There was a scurrying and a pattering of tiny feet and I shuddered at the thought of rats. There was plenty of mouldy food in those bins discarded from all the high-end restaurants around here.

Pulling my collar up tight around my neck, I held it there with a gloved hand as I walked, quickly approaching the building next door, a public house called The London Pride. Lights burned in every window and from the open doorway the strong smell of hops wreathed through the air. A couple of men stood outside smoking and making silly oohing noises while nudging each other as I walked past.

A figure suddenly materialised in front of me. I got a swift impression of a tan coat and a fedora hat, while trying to sidestep him as if we were dancing.

'Hey, Esther baby?' he said, reaching out and holding my arm to still me.

Even under the thick layer of jumper and coat, my arm felt scorched from his touch. Who was this person?

Glancing up, I saw with surprise that it was the Paul Newman lookalike as Martha had called him, the man who had been sitting with the bulldog woman earlier today watching me as I paraded up and down in all those wonderful outfits.

Even under the glow of a yellow street light, he was better looking than I remembered. His cheekbones were to die for, his lips full and kissable, and his eyes, wow, the bluest blue I'd ever seen. I was entranced by them and couldn't stop staring. They were as blue and clear as a summer sky with the twinkle of stars in there too. I was mesmerised.

'I was hoping to see you, Esther baby.'

'Go on mate, go for it,' catcalled the two men who still stood outside sucking on their cigarettes as if they were life lines.

'Paul Newman' immediately stepped towards them at which the two men hastily threw down their red-tipped stub ends and hurried inside.

I gave him a wry smile and said coldly, 'Esther Chambers actually,' coming to my senses and quickly averting my gaze from those baby-blues that for some strange reason had the power to suck me in. What was going on with me? I didn't even know this man.

'Ah, Esther Chambers, an intriguing name . . . is it your real name?'

'Of course,' I said quickly. 'Why would I give a false one?'

He shrugged. 'People do. Esther Chambers sounds like a name a girl would give herself who wanted, say, to be in films or to be a model . . .'

'It's my name,' I said icily, trying to move past him, but he moved too so we were right in front of each other, close enough to be almost touching.

He stared at me, his eyes raking my face as if he couldn't quite believe what he was seeing.

I said firmly, 'Please let me pass. I really must be getting home.'

I pulled my collar up tighter and shivered. It was turning cold now and the paths were frosted white and glimmering in the lamp light. The sky arching overhead was very black and sprinkled with stars and a sliver of moon.

'Do you know how extraordinarily beautiful you are?' he asked me. And before I could reply he chuckled and said, 'No you don't need to answer that. I suppose people, especially men, tell you that all the time, don't they?'

I nodded briefly and said, 'Look, I really do need to go home, it's getting dark and —'

'Yes . . . look . . . do you only model, or would you consider office work?' He proffered a packet of cigarettes to which I shook my head. He took one and, placing it between his full lips, lit it with a tiny gold lighter. He took a deep drag and, turning his head away from me, blew out a long thin plume of smoke reminding me of Pam earlier and her cigarette smoke. I got a sudden whiff of his spicy cologne as he moved.

A group of people walked past, laughing and chattering, and heading to the open door of the The London Pride. A man walking a dog on a lead shuffled past and a black cat walked nonchalantly across the road and disappeared with a yowl into the shadows.

Surprised at his question, I said, 'I'm a model, taking advantage of my looks before they fade.'

He smiled, showing teeth as bright white as his eyes were blue.

'I need an assistant. A secretary, I suppose you'd say, to help me in my business.'

'I went to college,' I told him proudly. 'I can type and take shorthand.'

He took another deep drag and turned his head again as he blew away the smoke, and then threw the stub down and ground it out with the heel of his smart black shoe.

'Come and work for me, then, Esther . . . I'll pay you more than you earn now, whatever that is. My offices are only a street or two away from here.'

'Are you crazy?' I said. 'I already told you, I'm a model! That's my job.'

'Yeah, but you said you can type and take shorthand! And maybe you fancy a change . . . what do they say? A change is as good as a rest?'

I smiled and said, 'I don't need a rest . . . and yeah, I got those qualifications in case I need them in my old age, like I said, when my looks are gone. After all, all models are beautiful and all secretaries are ugly, right?'

He laughed, his blue eyes flashing.

'Your looks will never fade. You're so beautiful it hurts.'

'Hurts?' I said. 'Wow, you are really crazy!'

'Yeah, it hurts my heart that I won't get to see that face every day.'

I shook my head, wanting to walk away and go home, but unable to for some reason. As if my slingbacks were stuck to the pavement with glue.

'Here, take my card, my number's on

it. Ring me if you change your mind.' He handed over a small business card held between the tips of two fingers. I took it from him, my hand letting go of my collar and revealing my lips that had been covered before.

'What's that?' he said, to my surprise putting out the tip of a finger and touching the place just above my upper lip. 'Not a flaw, surely. I thought you were perfect.'

'Don't,' I said, pushing his finger away. 'It's just a childhood scar.'

'It's a tiny cross,' he said, gazing at it intently. 'A tiny kiss.'

And before I knew what was happening, he leaned in close and kissed my scar.

I felt the brush of his stubble as his lips grazed my upper lip. It was as soft and as gentle as the whisper of an angel but I felt as if I'd been burned. Putting an arm around my waist, he pulled me closer and, as if in a daze I put my face up to his, and our lips met and held and parted. An erotic shiver ran down my spine.

'How dare you?' I said, pulling back from him, breathing hard as if I'd been running, raising my hand, so tempted was I to slap his face. 'I'm going home now, and don't even attempt to follow me or . . . I'll get the police on you.'

He looked disorientated, drugged almost, his lovely mouth moist.

'Ring me,' he said as I began to walk away. 'Any time, Esther, ring me . . .'

* * *

I hurried home through the darkening London streets, past tall houses where lamps shone brightly from large windows, past dark parks where trees clustered, outlined black like woolly blobs against the sky. Relief flooded through me as I turned into my road, Bleaker Street, where I rented a flat above a coffee bar called The Milk Maid.

I unlocked the back gate, slipped through, closed and locked it. I rushed up the stairs, my shoes clattering, unlocked, opened and closed the flat door quietly, standing with my back against it, and my heart beating fast.

After a while, I made my way into the sitting room and peered from between the curtains at the street below but there was nothing there, just a glittering empty path. A couple of sweet wrappers, a page of a newspaper blown along by the breeze. There was no one standing there staring up, looking for me, with those amazing baby blue eyes.

I giggled a bit at what I'd said. *I'll get the police on you* . . . I wondered what a policeman would have said if he found out I was complaining about the guy I'd been kissing minutes earlier.

I put the television on. There was no sound, the screen fuzzy with snow. What was it with the aerial in this building? I sat on the settee and smoothed out the card he'd given me, the card I'd carried screwed up in my hand. It was black with flashes of blue at the corners, his name and contact details clearly written in white lettering.

Jude Dunbar, Private Investigator, 3 Leadenhall Mansions, London W1, Tel: (01) 4389

I stared at the card for a long time, my mind working overtime. Then I put it with my bookmark inside the book that I was trying to read, *In Cold Blood* by Truman Capote.

After that I went to bed, but had trouble settling down and couldn't fall asleep for a very long time.

2

I was born Esther Fishbourne — Esther Rose Fishbourne — to very elderly parents for the time, being in their forties. Reginald and Mary Fishbourne. It was a snowy night in December, 1943.

'The snow was ten feet deep on the night you were born,' my dad was very fond of saying. 'We always said that you were delivered by the milkman on his horse-drawn float.'

'You were the best Christmas present I'd ever had,' Mum had always told me, her face one big beam of sunshine as she pulled me close, enveloping me in her warm arms, the smell of coal tar soap heavy in my nostrils. There were no frivolous perfumes for Mary Fishbourne in any way shape or form.

My dad, Reginald — Old Reg or Fishy to his mates in the office — worked for the council as a planning inspector, and would go off every morning, suited and booted and carrying a large leather brief-case. He was small and skinny and sported a great walrus moustache that he cultivated in front of the mirror as if it was a rare and exotic plant.

He would either walk or travel by bus to his offices on the Kings Road, preferring to use the car for leisure purposes only. He set off at the same time and arrived home at the same time every day.

'Like clockwork,' my mum always said. 'As reliable as the Changing of the Guard.' My mum, Mary, was a housewife, a fairly tall but round woman who wore her hair short and curly around a surprisingly youthful face. She was a bustling sort of woman, always on the move, and clad in a flowered wraparound pinny just like the one Martha wore. I very rarely saw her wearing anything else and if I did see her, for example, in her nightdress or her dressing gown, or even in a smart going-out dress, I always felt slightly scandalised. As if I didn't know who she was.

She bustled from the kitchen to the

dining room, from the dining room to the sitting room and from there she bustled upstairs to the bedrooms and the bathroom. She cleaned and polished and vacuumed and dusted, with what looked like a bunch of chicken feathers on a long wooden handle.

She scrubbed the front door and the step until they shone and polished the windows with newspaper until they gleamed, only stopping briefly for a bit of a gossip with Mrs Milner, our next door neighbour who had a lazy husband, seven kids and one on the way!

She cooked with flair on our tiny little stove. She made jams and chutneys and puddings and pies and we had a roast dinner not only on a Sunday, but during the week as well. Delectable smells that sneaked out of the kitchen and wreathed around the house greeted me every day when I came home tired and hungry from school.

When I was really little, she'd meet me in the playground. If I closed my eyes I could still picture her waiting for me, standing with all the other mums, wearing her good black coat and flat shoes, a black hat covering her curly hair.

The incessant beeping of the alarm clock awoke me and the vivid dream about Mum and Dad slowly faded as I open my eyes and realised where I was. No, I wasn't eighteen and still living at home in Norfolk Terrace but in my own flat, working as a model in a rather upmarket boutique and living the high life (well, for me anyway).

Reaching out blindly, lemon sunlight seeping around the edges of the curtains, I put out a hand to shut off the clock. Everything was quiet and still now, the room hushed; no noise from the coffee bar below, too early for that, but I could hear a faint rumbling of traffic passing by outside.

Thoughts of that man, the Paul Newman lookalike, ran through my mind and I touched the tiny scar above my lip, still feeling the burn of that kiss. A pleasant tingle ran through my body as I thought of it again and again.

Half-closing my eyes, I conjured up his face, and once again saw those cheekbones and lips and baby-blue eyes. I wondered if I'd ever see him again.

The smell of his cologne coiled through my mind until I felt as if I could smell it all around me and my heart raced with nerves.

What is wrong with me? How can a man make me feel this way? I need to curb these feelings.

From the limited experience I'd had with men, I'd realised there was only one thing they saw in me and that was my looks. Oh yeah, it was great to be pretty, to a certain extent, but in other ways it was a hindrance.

Thoughts of such an unlikely job offer ran through my mind and, reaching for my book from the bedside cabinet, I slipped the card he'd given me from between the pages and read it again.

Jude Dunbar, Private Investigator. Was he different from the others? Did he think I would make a good secretary to a private investigator? That I could use my brains and not my looks?

My spirits rose at the thought. Then I remembered he'd said, 'Do you know how extraordinarily beautiful you are?' and my heart sank.

Slipping out of bed and reaching for my dressing gown, pushing my feet into fluffy heeled mules, I wandered into the kitchen and filled the kettle, placing it on the stove top which lit with a pop and a smell of sulphur. The Beatles blared from the radio as I switched it on.

'Help! I need somebody. Help! Not just anybody, Help! You know I need someone, Help! When I was younger, so much younger than today, I never needed anybody's help in any way . . .'

The kettle shrieked to the boil, drowning out The Beatles and filling the kitchen with steam.

Sipping my coffee and jigging from foot to foot to the music, I gazed from the window at the street below. People walked past on their way to work, men wearing suits and ties, women wearing mini-skirts and high boots, belted trench coats and ponchos, small groups of children wearing school uniform, satchels hanging from their shoulders and ties askew.

People wobbled along on bicycles and a Mini cruised by closely followed by a VW Beetle and, I think, a Morris Minor. I wasn't very good on cars but I knew a Mini and a VW Beetle when I saw one . . . cars to die for, oh and the Bubble Car too. What did the advert say? *Car comfort at motorcycle running cost.*

Yeah, I was saving for one of those. I just had to pass my driving test first.

I glance at my watch realising I'd have to get a move on if I was to get to work on time. As I did so, an sudden awful spurt of guilt shot through me bringing back a memory of Mum and Dad giving me this very watch for my eighteenth birthday at a get-together for my friends at our house. Excitedly I had opened the box to find an Ingersoll, small and delicate, when I'd always yearned for an Omega.

I'd felt a stab of irritation at bumbling old Dad and bustling old Mum in front of all my friends who had young, trendy parents. Being called Esther Fishbourne didn't help either. I felt as though the surname and the watch didn't go with my young life of good looks and trendy clothes.

Neither of them said anything, they were their usual charming selves to me and everyone there who'd come to celebrate, but I had a feeling they both knew. I tried so hard to make it up to them . . . and then suddenly they were gone and it was too late.

⋆ ⋆ ⋆

A frantic banging on the door brought me out of my reverie along with a voice hollering as loud as could be.

'Hey Esther baby, what ya doing? You should be on your way to the shop by now. I've been waiting on the corner . . . you sick or something?'

Yes, I thought, wishing I'd never had

the memory. *Sick to the bottom of my heart*. Pushing the thoughts away, I rushed to the door to let in an irate Martha.

'Oh my God, you're not even dressed yet! Have you bathed? Honey, I'll run you your bath . . .'

'I'm not sick, Martha, just running late. Sorry.'

She squeezed my shoulder as she bustled past me into the bathroom and I heard the sound of running water and smelled lavender, wild and heady, as she added bath oil.

'Are we on water rations?' I asked as I splashed around in what looked like a puddle at the bottom of the bath tub. She giggled and I heard the familiar sound of the kettle boiling, music played. *I got flowers in the spring, I got you to wear my ring* . . . I hummed along to the tune, a picture coming into my mind again of the Paul Newman lookalike, and the lure of those mesmerising blue eyes, making my whole body shiver. I raised my shoulders to my ears in ecstasy as I soaped my body with a sponge, squeezing out water that ran in little rivers along my breasts and over my flat stomach.

'Yeah well, it don't grow on trees, Esther baby,' said Martha, her voice close to the bathroom door.

And when I'm sad, you're a clown, and when I get scared, you're always around . . .

I dressed carefully in a black and white shift dress with white tights and black boots. I made up my eyes, thick and black, and slicked pale pink on my lips. I belted my coat tight around my waist as Martha and I clattered down the stairs and out into the fresh air of the cold March morning.

A long white van was parked outside right on the kerb and a young guy, all muscles and tight T-shirt, busy unloading supplies for the coffee bar. He did a double take when he saw me and, not looking where he was going, bumped into a group of kids idling along, a transistor radio held between them, belting out the Stones.

I can't get no satisfaction, cause I try and

I try and I try and I try . . . I can't get no . . . satisfaction . . .

'Hey, mister,' complained one of the kids shaking a chubby fist.

Disorientated, the guy said, 'Hey . . . uh, sorry, kids.' He blushed a deep red and, hiding himself behind a great pallet of bread, scurried through The Milk Maid's open door.

Martha laughed long and loud, nudging me.

'See? The men are putty in your hands.'

A red double decker bus trundled past, gloomy faces staring from the window, the conductor hanging on at the back, his money bag and ticket machine criss crossed over his chest. I suddenly felt glad to be alive with such a blue sky arching above. Trees were budding, their soft green leaves unfurling like a precious secret, and daffodils and tulips blossomed in parks and gardens in patches of red and gold.

Food smells lingered in the air from nearby restaurants, something spicy and hot reminding me of my favourite Vesta beef curry. Dust rose up in little dry puffs beneath our feet as we walked.

Catcalls and wolf whistles rang out in our direction from a group of workmen who, grey with dust, turned a dull red when Martha shouted at them to knock it off. She nodded, pleased with herself, as we reached Attitude and let ourselves in through the back door and up the stone steps to the dressing rooms.

The communal room was quiet and empty, tidy too . . . for once.

'Do you know who you remind me of?' I asked as I put my bag down in the small make up area and shrugged off my coat.

'Who?' she asked in her I-don't-care-what-you-think tone, tying her flowery pinny around her ample waist and pulling it tight. She walked to the rack and rifled through the clothes hanging there, umming and aahing, pushing them this way and that, holding items up to the light searching for marks and stains.

'Scarlett O'Hara's Mammy!'

'Really?' She looked over her shoulder at me, her chubby face split into a grin. 'Well, ain't that a good thing? She was a good, strong person, didn't put up with no nonsense. Yeah, I can see why you think that, Esther baby...'

I was just about to reply when Mrs Rodgers, the owner of Attitude, walked through the door closely followed by Jane and Pam.

'Morning, Esther,' said Mrs Rodgers. 'Hi there, Martha.'

Martha bobbed her head and I said, 'Morning Mrs Rodgers.' She checked her watch before nodding towards Jane and Pam. Luckily they were just on time. She was a stickler for timekeeping. There was no sign of Julie which was nothing new.

A tall, bony woman with long, black hair like a Sindy doll, Mrs Rodgers wore the shortest mini skirts I'd ever seen, even more mini than a mini. Today was no exception as I could tell by the expression on Martha's face.

'Esther? There's a couple in the shop

asking for you.' She pointed towards the rail where Martha still stood, idly flicking through the clothes, while listening in, her ears poised like a bat, 'The outfits they want modelling are there. Second time this week you've been asked for specifically. Well done.' She smiled, all teeth in her bony face.

My heart rose and started clattering away like a freight train at the thought of who it might be and baby blue eyes swam into my mind. I couldn't wait to put the first outfit on and model it for him, for without a doubt, it had to be the Paul Newman lookalike, Jude Dunbar. No one else had asked for me by name.

It didn't cross my mind that maybe it was a bit too soon for him and the bulldog woman to be back here for more clothes.

'Eww,' said Pam as Mrs Rodgers sashayed out of the room. 'You can see her underwear . . . without her even bending down.'

She and Jane pulled wooden chairs up to their mirrors and, clattering the make-up from their bags onto the little shelf in front of them, got to work on their faces. Jane began to apply foundation with a sponge, smoothing it out over her nose and cheeks and temples as if she was painting a wall.

'Yeah,' Martha said, turning away from the clothes rail, and putting her hands on her hips, 'A mini's a mini but . . .'

Suddenly Julie came bursting through the door.

'Morning — sorry I'm so late. My cat had kittens last night! I just told Mrs Rodgers, but she's not happy.'

'Bring them with you did you, honey?' drawled Pam. 'For evidence?'

'Hey . . . you haven't got a cat!' Jane exclaimed, a frown furrowing her forehead.

All three of them laughed and Martha shook her head. Julie always had outlandish stories as to why she was late.

'Help me today, Martha?' asked Pam, giving me the dead eye. Martha did a grim pressing together of her lips while folding her arms across her ample chest and stared her out, no problem.

'What's the first outfit, Martha?' I asked briskly, stepping behind the blood-red curtain to get changed. I began pulling off my clothes as Martha, putting her hand through a gap in the curtain, gave me a mini dress. It was all purple and yellow swirls and curls on a white background with a ruffled hem that caressed my thighs as I pranced out into the shop, my face wearing a neutral expression, getting ready to see 'Paul Newman' and the bulldog again.

Mrs Rodgers had the radio on today and Lulu singing *Shout* echoed around the shop as I sashayed around.

My neutral face was gone, replaced not by smiles as I had hoped, but a wry twist to my lips. I'd seen not the Paul Newman lookalike and the 'bulldog' as I'd thought I would, but a young laid-back hippy couple whom I'd never seen before. They gave the peace sign after every dress change and told Mrs Rodgers how far out it was that Grace Kelly modelled for them because, in their own words, 'Hey man, we thought she was just in the movies.'

3

The music was deafening and thumping. I could feel it pulsing beneath my feet and reverberating through my body, as I leaned in closer to Julie so I could hear what she was saying.

Big girls don't cry . . .

People were jostling all around us, and the smell of so many different perfumes mingled with sweat and alcohol, hanging in the air. I recognised Estee Lauder's Youth Dew straight away for its strong, spicy aroma.

Julie got as close as she could to my ear and said, 'There's a really cute guy over there. Do you mind if I go and talk to him?'

I shook my head and mouthed 'of course not' and then took a sip of my drink, some sort of fruity cocktail that was going to my head more than I wanted it to. I watched Julie slink away and perch like an exotic bird, in her tight red cat suit with a little piece of frippery, a black chiffon scarf tied in a bow around her neck, on a high stool next to a guy with long black hair tied back in a pony-tail.

He looked a bit taken aback at her sudden appearance but ordered her a drink, something dark, only about two inches in a tall glass that she knocked back straight away. I noticed that he wore a couple of heavy gold rings on his fingers which I thought unusual on a man.

The barman, a heavy-set guy with a bald head, a tattoo of a snake winding its way up his arm, stared amazed as she asked for another.

I felt a bit conspicuous now, standing alone, and my black mini dress and boots seemed a little too revealing. I wore large gold hoop earrings and my eye make-up was thick and black with only a faint colour on my lips. I wasn't used to going out partying and definitely not to places like this, places that I'd always thought of as being 'dens of iniquity' as my Dad had always told me.

'Soho?' he would have exclaimed. 'No, not my Esther!'

But hey, here I was in Soho, in a club called Milly's. Jane, Pam, Julie and I had followed hordes of people down steep stone steps into this wonderful cavern of flashing lights and music, where there was a long, ornate bar and comfy leather seating that hugged the walls, as well as low tables and stools scattered about like little mushrooms. The small dance floor was packed with hot, writhing bodies.

I was getting furtive glances from men passing by and wished that Jane or Julie, or even Pam, would hurry up and come back, although that seemed very unlikely now. I could still see Julie with the guy with the ponytail, and they were chatting to the barman now, but there was no sign of the other two. They'd both disappeared almost straight away, Pam already a bit tipsy from drinks at the pub beforehand. I wouldn't even be here if Pam hadn't invited me, making it seem like some sort of challenge when at first

I'd said no; that I didn't go to places like that, not on a work night.

She'd ridiculed me in front of the others, teasingly calling me a Mummy's girl, a Daddy's girl, and even though I still didn't want to go, I caved in and said yes, all the time with the familiar pain in my heart at the mention of their names. But I realised that she didn't know — no one did.

Martha berated me all the way back to Bleaker Street, saying I gave in too easily.

'Maybe it's time, Martha,' was all I could think to say to her. 'Maybe it's time to stop locking myself away . . .' A song ran through my head, *Please lock me away, and don't allow the day here inside, where I hide with my loneliness* . . .

Just when I'm on the verge of finishing my drink and getting out of there, I hear a voice at my side.

'Do you come here often, love?'

He was short, at least a foot shorter than me and had a mop of blond curly hair and a sweet baby face that lit up in a smile as he said, 'Cor, you're really pretty . . .'

I smiled at him and took another sip of my drink, my head spinning now as I swayed to the music. *Imagine me and you, I do, I think about you day and night, it's only right . . .*

'Wanna dance?' He started swaying about opposite me, his arms bent and his hands in fists, as if he was preparing for the boxing ring. I couldn't help but giggle.

To think about the girl you love, and hold her tight, so happy together . . .

I drained my glass and set it down on the table. Baby Face lurched forward and said into my ear, 'I'll get you another drink, love, what you having?'

'I don't know what it is . . .' I slurred, trying hard not to, but feeling dizzy and out of sorts, the room revolving. 'Some sort of cocktail, I think.'

He sniffed at the glass and said, 'Smells like Bacardi to me . . . I'll get ya summit . . . you wait here, OK?' He moved away and then stopped and turned.

'Don't you move, OK?'

I nodded and watched him as he was sucked into the crowds at the bar and disappeared.

I can't see me loving nobody but you for all my life, when you're with me, baby the sky will be blue for all my life . . .

'Esther?'

His hand gripped my arm, sending a warmth coursing through my body that I didn't even know existed before.

'You!' I said, staring straight into a pair of blue eyes, eyes that were as blue as the sky on a hot summer day. 'Ol' blue eyes…' I couldn't quite believe he was there right next to me.

He threw his head back and laughed so I could see the whole long column of his neck and throat. A long black overcoat hung open from his shoulders and he wore a dark hat pushed back on his head.

'Hey, are you tipsy? Come on, I'll take you outside for some fresh air.' He put a protective arm around my shoulders, pulling me so close I could smell the spicy cologne emanating from his skin.

The only one for me is you, and you for me, so happy together . . .

We walked down the steps, the music getting fainter and fainter. *I can't see me loving nobody but you for all my life* . . . People were walking up, hot bodies lurching into us and knocking us against the cold stone wall, and then we were outside and I took several deep breaths of fresh air until the dizziness went away and the whole world stopped revolving.

I shivered, shrugging my shoulders to my ears. He said, 'Here...' and took off his warm overcoat and draped it around my shoulders. Underneath he wore a dark suit, the jacket open and the top buttons of his shirt undone, showing a dense mat of chest hair.

I averted my gaze because my heart was clattering away so hard, I thought I might faint. He put his arm around my shoulders again and pulled me up close to his warm body.

'What are you doing here?'

'I came with friends from work,' I told

him. 'But they all disappeared . . .' And then as I suddenly remembered the boy inside the club, 'Oh no, Baby Face went to get me a drink . . . what will he say if I'm not there?'

'Baby Face? What — Baby Face Nelson, the bank robber?'

'No!' I giggled. 'A boy, well he looked like a boy. He went to get me another drink.'

He shook his head. 'I wouldn't recommend you have any more. Not used to alcohol, are you?'

I shook my head. He tapped a cigarette from a crumpled packet and put one between his lips. I couldn't stop staring at his lips, at the cigarette and his lips.

'You want one?' He held out the packet.

I shook my head and he said, 'No, I didn't think you smoked.' He lit up with the little gold lighter. Taking a deep drag, he turned his head, blowing the smoke away from me. 'It's a dirty habit, but pretty addictive.'

'Where's your wife?' I demanded accusingly.

He frowned and shook his head, looking straight at me. 'I don't have a wife.'

'But what about . . . ?'

'The woman I was with at the shop?'

'Yes.'

'Ah, she's my aunt, on my mother's side, the eldest of four. Likes to take my advice on clothes.' Then he added, 'Name's Maud. They're all M's. Maud, Marilyn, Milly and Miranda.'

I smiled as I thought how close Martha had been in her assumption about Jude and his companion. *Some guy's just come in with a woman looks old enough to be his mother* . . .

'Wow, that's amazing! Which is your mum?'

'Marilyn. Their maiden name was Morris, so all double Ms . . . their Mum and Dad too, Maurice and Matilda.' He gave a small chuckle.

My brain whirred. 'So your grandad was called Maurice Morris?'

'Yeah . . . a confusing name, but he

liked it, used it as a party piece. Hey, you worked that out quickly. Brains as well as beauty.' He gave me a sly wink. 'I knew I was right in offering you the job.'

There was a short silence while he smoked, and I didn't reply, when he suddenly said, 'There was a wife though . . . once, a long time ago…'

'There was?' I turned to gaze at him. 'What happened?'

'Divorced,' he said carelessly. 'We weren't married for long.'

'Why? What happened?'

He shrugged. 'She met somebody else and moved across the pond.'

'Which pond?'

'To America, of course,' he said, laughing at me. 'Surely you know what 'across the pond' means?'

'Oh, of course,' I said, not knowing at all really. 'Didn't you want to go there? Across the pond, I mean?'

'What — with her and her new chap? A threesome, huh?'

I giggled as he went on, 'I wouldn't have wanted to go anyway. I'd just set up my own business, the business I have now, here in London. I'd worked for someone else for a long time and wanted to strike out on my own. I'd never have gone across the pond at that time, not for anyone.'

'So she went with someone else?'

'Yeah, pretty much.' And before I could ask anything else, 'How about we get a cup of coffee? There's a great little place on Bleaker Street called The Milk Maid that's open late.' He looked at me, his baby blues glowing in the harsh yellow of the street light. 'Well, Esther . . . how about it?'

I gazed at his lovely face and said yes.

* * *

Pam didn't look good when Martha and I arrived at work the following morning. Her beautiful green eyes were bloodshot and she was definitely hungover, drooping in front of the mirror like a wilted flower. She sipped morosely at black coffee, a look of sick despair on her face.

I was surprised she was there before me — or there at all, to tell you the truth.

Jane was busy making up her face but, as usual, there was no sign of Julie. She'd no doubt hurry in later, hair dishevelled and make-up smeared, saying that her pet dog had caught rabies and attacked her in the night so she couldn't get up this morning. Oh yeah, the more weird the excuse the better for Julie.

'You better get the first customers today, Esther baby,' said Pam in a croaky old man's smoking voice. 'I need time to recover.' She sniffed hard and swallowed two little white pills with a sip of coffee, offering a nasty aside as she did so. 'You'll probably be summoned anyway, seeing as you're the pretty little favourite.'

'Watch your mouth, lady,' snapped Martha, and then made some comment under her breath about people that smoked too much. Pam viciously rounded on her saying, 'Mind your own business, old woman.'

'It's OK, Martha,' I said, laying a gentle hand on her shoulder before she went in for the kill. 'Sticks and stones and all that.' I pushed my bag into my locker but didn't lock it — no one ever did. I left the key swinging idly from the little metal door.

Jane, so used to Pam's digs and insults to me, carried on placidly with her make-up, only commenting that Julie was even later than usual and would catch it from Mrs Rodgers when she did turn up.

'There's only so much that woman will take,' she said gravely.

I didn't care this morning, though. I felt that I could cope with any crisis that was thrown at me. Nothing could pierce this feeling of wellbeing, this Jude Dunbar cocoon I'd wrapped myself in.

The morning flew by with plenty of customers coming in and I modelled non-stop, my head in the clouds. The Paul Newman lookalike Jude Dunbar was never far from my mind, his face hovering like a disembodied ghost.

Mrs Rodgers had music blasting out

of the speakers today, pretty raunchy too, as I strutted my stuff around the shop floor. *All I'm askin' is for a little respect, when you come home (hey baby)*.

Pam must have felt mostly recovered because I got a glimpse of her from the corner of my eye shimmying up and down in a red mini skirt, gladiator sandals wrapped around her legs like barbed wire. I saw Jane too but, even as the morning progressed, there was no sign of Julie on the shop floor.

'Yeah, but we're all covering for her now,' I heard Pam say as I stepped back into the changing room later that afternoon.

'What? Still no sign of Julie?' I asked.

Martha shook her head as I ducked between the curtains and she helped unzip my dress. Tying a robe tightly around my waist I sat at a mirror and began creaming my face, rubbing lightly at mascara and lipstick with my fingers until it began to disappear.

'No, she hasn't turned up yet, Esther,' said Jane. 'We're all pretty worried now.'

Yeah, except Pam, I thought. *She seems more annoyed about her not being there than worried.*

'Did you see her home?' Jane persisted.

'No.' I shook my head as I took a cotton wool ball and began to smooth the cream from my face. I peered closer into the mirror. 'She was sitting at the bar with a guy with long hair tied in a ponytail when I left.'

'Who was he? What's his name?' asked Pam, looking at me as if it was my fault that Julie was late and maybe still with this unknown guy. She still looked washed out, her face drawn and pale, but greatly improved since this morning. I met her eye in the mirror.

'I don't know. I don't think she knew him either. She just sat herself down next to him and that was that.' There was a silence. 'I think he bought her a couple of drinks though.'

Mrs Rodgers suddenly hustled into the room, pushing through the door as if she was mad at someone. She had a real big frown on her face as she said, 'OK girls, which one of you didn't put the pink flowered gown aside for Mrs Lewis? I have an irate customer out in the front wanting to know where her parcel is.'

'I put it right here on the rack when it'd been modelled,' said Martha, flicking through the clothes with a skilled hand. It was standard practice that a customer could buy a garment at a reduced price if it had been modelled in the shop.

'Well, it ain't there now,' said Mrs Rodgers in her quiet but deadly voice. 'Who modelled it?'

'I did,' I told her, turning from the mirror, my face clear of make-up now but no less beautiful, I knew that for sure. A fleeting look of hatred passed over Pam's face, taking my breath away.

'Yeah, didn't you know?' she said to Mrs Rodgers. 'Martha doesn't pick up for anyone but her Esther baby now.'

'OK,' said Mrs Rodgers, glaring at me. 'Where's the gown, Esther?'

Feeling confused and flushing a bright

red, I said, 'I don't know.' I cast my mind back over all the clothes I'd modelled that morning but couldn't remember this gown in particular. Anyway, as Martha said, she'd have put it on the rail before giving me the next outfit.

Glancing at my locker, the key swinging from the lock, I saw that it was now closed when I'd definitely left it slightly open this morning, and my bag was on the table.

'I put my bag in my locker this morning,' I said. 'What's it doing sitting out here on the table?'

Hands on my hips, I glanced around at everyone. 'What's going on?'

Pam averted her gaze and Jane looked worried but no one spoke. How I wished Julie was here.

Mrs Rodgers went to the locker and pulled at the key. It was locked.

'Hey, leave that locker alone,' said Martha. 'Only Esther should go in there.'

Reaching past Mrs Rodgers, I put out a shaky hand and turned the key. The metal door opened with a creak and I glanced inside. I wasn't surprised at what I saw.

I could hear music blaring from the shop, *And when I touch you I feel happy inside . . .*

'Ah, so there it is,' said Mrs Rodgers, nodding with a satisfied smile pasted on her face as she peered over my shoulder. 'The pink gown, eh?'

Snaking my hand into the cool depths of the locker, I pulled the gown out, feeling the softness and slipperiness of it against my skin as I shook my head.

'I didn't put this in here, Mrs Rodgers. You know full well I wouldn't steal from you.'

It's such a feeling that my love I can't hide, I can't hide . . .

'Oh yeah, and how do I know that then, Esther?' She snatched the gown away from me and made to go out of the room. 'I'll talk to you about this later.'

'I'm not a thief,' I said through gritted teeth.

'No, she ain't no thief!' shouted Martha, hands on her hips and her head pushed forward like a bellowing bull.

'Shut up, you,' said Mrs Rodgers, pointing a long bony finger at Martha. 'Esther, I'll deal with you later.'

Suddenly coming to a decision and standing proud and tall, I said, 'No, you won't deal with me later, Mrs Rodgers. If you think I'm a thief then I'm going now.' I slipped behind the curtain and started to get dressed, Martha helping me to zip up. Tying my coat tightly at the waist, I pushed past Mrs Rodgers still standing in the doorway, her mouth gaping open, clutching the pink flowered gown to her breasts like a shield. I slung my bag over one shoulder.

'And I quit too,' said Martha, following on behind me, trying to button her coat and lug her heavy bag all at the same time.

'Oh for goodness sake, stop now . . . you can't leave me with just two models, with Julie not being here either . . . *Esther!*'

Her voice rang out after us like a foghorn.

I vaguely heard Jane's voice.

'Esther, please come back . . . don't go . . . Martha, tell her...'

We walked out into the bright day, blinking like moles coming up out of the earth.

'Martha, you can't quit too. Please go back,' I implored her. A cool wind gusted around my legs making me shiver.

'No,' she said stubbornly. 'I ain't workin' there without you, Esther baby.'

'But what about money?' I watched her face carefully, the wrinkles around her eyes and her mouth more pronounced in the glare of the sun.

'George can look after me for a while. It's the least he can do!'

Martha had a husband who worked nights as a printer at a big London newspaper. She'd never mentioned children.

'I know it was Pam,' I said, as we got to the corner of Bleaker Street.

Martha shrugged. 'Who else could it be? She has a real downer on you, Esther baby. But you wait and see, Mrs Rodgers will come looking for you, that's for sure. You're too big a draw for her to lose, especially if Julie doesn't turn up again.'

'Julie will turn up,' I said. 'Why wouldn't she?'

Martha shrugged again.

'Let me know if you go back there. I'll only go back if you do. Here, this is my telephone number.' She delved into her bag and produced a notebook and a pen.

'Wow . . . you've got a telephone in your flat?'

'Yeah . . . who would have thought it, eh? Martha Engleson with a telephone! I reached the dizzy heights.'

I tucked the folded piece of paper into the little front pocket of my bag.

'Call me, huh?' She made to walk away but stopped and said, 'I'll tell you what though, Esther baby, I put that gown on the rack when you took it off.'

I nodded. I knew that Martha would never let me down. I watched her walk away, a small, round figure in her good black coat reminding me in some ways of Mum waiting patiently with all the other mums in the school playground all those years ago.

4

I sneaked up the stairs to my flat, not wanting Tony or any Milk Maid customers to see me home so early. I put down my bag and shrugged off my coat, feeling as down as I ever had.

Walking out of my job had taken more out of me than I cared to admit. I could hear the heavy thump, thump of the jukebox from the coffee bar below and the smell of bacon and something else frying — chips and maybe eggs — seeped through the cracks in the door.

I hadn't eaten lunch because of the disruption at work, so was desperate for coffee — food I couldn't face at the moment. I went into the kitchen and lit the gas to boil the kettle.

What to do now? I needed a job, otherwise how would I pay the rent? I had savings and money in stocks and shares, but I didn't want to go into that. Huh, I bet Mum and Dad were laughing at me now. They hated my plans to move to the other side of London (as if it was Australia!) and be a model. Dad wanted me to apply for an admin post in the council so we could travel to and from work together every day.

Suddenly Jude Dunbar's voice echoed through my head. *Come and work for me, Esther, I'll pay you more than you earn now . . . whatever that is.*

Well, I wasn't that desperate yet. Pen-pushing wasn't for me. I'd do a tour of the boutiques and department stores tomorrow. Live models were much sought after so I was sure someone somewhere would take me on; after all, I had my looks and experience now too.

Attitude boutique always seemed to be a cut above other places but, then again, if the owner called you a thief knowing full well that you weren't . . . maybe it wasn't such a good place to work after all.

I sank back into the settee and took a sip of coffee, my thoughts wandering to the evening before and of course Jude

Dunbar, and the expression on his face when he realised I already knew about The Milk Maid café and, in fact, lived in the flat above. I no longer thought of him as the Paul Newman lookalike but as Jude. Confiding in someone, telling them your deepest secrets, can quickly put you on first name terms, and gazing into those baby blues felt so right. I was sure that, if I wasn't very careful, Jude Dunbar could occupy a very special place in my heart. I needed to keep him at arm's length, that was for sure.

'Hmm,' I could imagine Martha saying with her ever-ready wit. 'Depends how long your arms are, Esther baby.'

'Hey, Esther!' I heard a sudden shout from below. 'Telephone . . . hey, you up there?' A pounding of feet on the stairs was followed by a tap at the door. 'Esther . . . telephone…'

It was Tony, owner of The Milk Maid, his face flushed from the kitchen.

'Hey, Esther, making me come all the way up here . . . I got customers in, I'm cooking.' He raised his palms. 'You're lucky I answered the call. Now, if you weren't so pretty...'

I felt like saying, 'Tony, the rent money should cover the cost of a private telephone, then you wouldn't have to answer my calls.'

Instead I said, 'Sorry, Tony,' as I followed him down the steps and went to the pay phone that clung to the wall in the hallway like a shiny black beetle. The receiver hung down on the end of its cord, still swinging slightly, from where Tony had left it.

'Hello?'

'Esther?' My heart sank, it was Mrs Rodgers, I'd recognise that deep nasal voice anywhere.

'If this is about me coming back I—'

'No, not that . . . not at the moment. I need you to come to the shop, though.'

'Why?'

'We had a call . . . about Julie.'

'Julie? Is she all right?'

'Well, we don't know. You gotta talk to the police. They had a call from her room-mate, Alice someone or other. She said Julie didn't come home last night, her bed hasn't been slept in. She didn't know what to do so I called the police. You might have been the last person to see her in that club you all went to. It's either you come here or I give the police your address —'

'No,' I said immediately, thinking of Tony and the customers in The Milk Maid and their reaction if the police turned up wanting me for questioning, however innocent of any wrongdoing I was. Tony would have a fit. He might even ask me to leave. 'I'll come to the shop.'

My heart thumping hard, I slipped on my boots and shrugged on my coat, tying it tightly at the waist as I ran down the steps, my bag dangling from my shoulder, cold hands stuffed in my pockets, and made the short journey to Attitude. It was dusk now and cold; even the stars looked like chips of ice scattered all over the darkening sky.

A police car was parked discreetly on the cobbled street at the side of the building. Hoping and praying that Julie had come to no harm, but had perhaps gone home with the guy with the long dark ponytail, I opened the staff door and clattered up the stairs into the shop.

⋆ ⋆ ⋆

'Here, drink this . . . your hands are freezing, Esther. Where are your gloves?' Jude Dunbar leaned across the table in The Milk Maid café and handed me a mug of hot coffee. I glanced at him from under my lashes, at his face, taking it all in, his sculpted cheekbones, those lovely blue eyes, and couldn't believe he was here waiting for me when I got back from Attitude after 'helping the police with their enquiries' as they say.

'I forgot my gloves,' I told him. 'And my scarf. I was too worried about Julie to realise I didn't have them with me.' I winced as, taking a sip of coffee, I burnt my lip.

'Julie's still not turned up?' he asked.

I shook my head. 'I told them

everything I know. I saw her talking to a guy with a long ponytail — oh, and the barman — at Milly's last night . . . and then I left with you.'

'Did you tell them my name?'

'No, I said I left with a friend. They didn't ask your name. Is that odd, do you think?'

He took a sip of coffee and shrugged.

'Maybe not at this stage. If time goes by and Julie doesn't turn up, they may want more evidence that you had nothing to do with her disappearance, and might then want me to vouch for you!'

'Huh, as if I'd have anything to do with Julie disappearing! Julie is more of a friend than either Jane or Pam.'

'Yeah, well, they don't know you from Adam . . . or Eve, I should say. You might turn out to be the first female London serial killer for all they know.'

The door pinged open, letting in a burst of cold air. A couple walked in just as the jukebox whirred and clicked and Tom Jones started singing, '*What's new, pussycat? . . . woah, wo-o-o-ah . . .*'

'As if today wasn't bad enough without Julie going missing.' He looked at me questioningly so I filled him in on the saga of the pink flowered dress. I noticed the couple that had come in sit down at a nearby table. Tony brought menus over and cups of steaming coffee. I heard him telling them his bacon and eggs were the best in the whole of London while they looked on wide-eyed.

Pussycat, pussycat, I've got flowers and lots of hours to spend with you . . .

Jude took off his hat, putting it on the table between us, and loosened his coat. Leaning forward so that his lips were inches from mine he said, 'Don't go back, Esther, come and work with me. I've got several good cases on at the moment. Maybe we can find Julie too — or at least get enough evidence to take to the police.'

Pussycat, pussycat, I love you, yes I do . . . you and your pussycat nose . . .

'I'll pay you more than you're earning, whatever it is. In fact, name your price.'

'Mrs Rodgers has asked me to go back. But I can't get out of my head that she thought I was a thief — and, as well as that, I don't think I can work with Pam again.'

'You're a good draw for her, Esther, that's why she wants you. If you are thinking of going back, make her wait.' He stared at me with those disconcerting blue eyes. 'Name your price then?'

'What will you expect of me?'

Pussycat, pussycat, you're so thrilling and I'm so willing to care for you . . .

He grinned and his blue eyes sparkled like jewels as he said, 'I don't know whether there's any innuendo in that question, Esther, but I need reports typing up and, of course, help with the investigations. Two heads are better than one — don't you think?'

I drained the last drop of coffee, my mug to my face to hide my blushes. The grounds tasted bitter in my mouth as I said, 'I'd like to be appreciated for my brains, Jude, and work with you on an equal footing.'

'You're on! Please, Esther, don't go back to Attitude. Come and work with me. You'll find it interesting — plenty of action but, obviously, mundane sometimes too.'

Tony put plates overflowing with bacon and eggs in front of the couple he'd coerced into buying, just as the door pinged again and a group of teenagers dressed in jeans and sweatshirts came flooding in. Tony's wife, Marie, had turned up now, getting ready to serve, tying an apron around her waist.

'As most jobs are,' I said. 'OK, a trial period . . . say a couple of months?'

'Six months and you're on.'

I hesitated but only for a split second.

'OK, six months it is.'

'Seal the deal?'

I held out my hand but, oh no, Jude Dunbar had other thoughts. Standing up and grabbing my arm, he pulled me away from the table so that nothing stood between us. Our bodies slotted together perfectly like the missing piece of a jigsaw puzzle and his mouth fitted perfectly too, his lips soft yet hard against mine.

Pussycat, pussycat, I love you, yes I do! You and your pussycat eyes . . .

Vaguely I heard Tony saying, 'Hey, Esther, come on, why here? You only live upstairs . . .'

* * *

I awoke suddenly, the impact of the crash still fresh in my mind. Instinctively I put a hand to my upper lip where the piece of jagged glass from the windscreen had been, stuck into my skin like a spear, giving me the scar I still wore today. My clock, glowing bright green in the dark, showed three am.

Gazing around the bedroom, my eyes gradually becoming accustomed to the dim light, a feeling of dread stole through my body. It had been another day and still no sign of Julie. Jude wanted me to go with him to the nightclub, Milly's, to see if we could track down the guy with the long dark ponytail. The police had run into a brick wall and needed all the help they could get to find out where she was.

Getting out of bed I padded to the kitchen, poured a glass of cold water and, sipping it, went back to bed. I'd told Jude about the crash — something I'd never told anyone before.

'Yeah,' he said. 'I guessed you changed your name. Remember I asked and you said you hadn't? And the scar –' He put out a finger and touched it gently. 'You lied about that, too.'

Even now, four years later, I still feel it was my fault — that I shouldn't have told them my plans on our way to the restaurant when Dad was driving, but afterwards when we were safe at home. It was my eighteenth birthday, a foggy, snowy night in December. There was ice on the roads and the trees looked like bones etched against the sky.

I couldn't wait to tell them. I was proud of myself; I had a job and somewhere to live, and maybe they could have accepted that. It was the name change they really didn't like. I didn't think it would mean so much to them but, if I wanted to be successful as a model, how could I be called Esther Fishbourne? People don't seem to realise how much there is in a name.

I remember Dad saying in an unusually harsh voice, 'What's wrong with your surname, Esther?' and Mum putting a comforting hand on his knee as, for a split second, he turned his head towards me. The other car appeared as if from nowhere and, bam, it was over — for all of us. I had a feeling they'd gone even before the ambulance came. For a long time I'd wished I'd gone too.

Putting my glass on the bedside cabinet, I lay down, pulling the covers up to my neck with a cold hand. I closed my eyes and drifted, dreaming vividly on and off, until I awoke to Jude banging on the door telling me to get up, ready for work.

* * *

It seemed wrong to be in Milly's night-club during the day. It looked seedy and down-at-heel without its night-time glamour, like an actor without the Hollywood sheen. A few solitary men sat drinking and a group of young men played a raucous game of cards. The smell of hops and sweat hung in the air. The music was still loud, filling every corner and making conversation so difficult that the young girl serving at the bar had to get extremely close to Jude when he asked if the barman with a snake tattoo on his arm was working today.

I've got sunshine on a cloudy day, when it's cold outside I've got the month of May . . .

Chewing listlessly, insolently looking Jude up and down, she said, 'Oh, you mean Dennis?'

I didn't like her attitude so leaned in close to her and said, 'If Dennis has a bald head and a snake tattoo on his arm then, yes, it's Dennis we want to talk to.'

She had black-rimmed eyes and wore a plunging neckline that showed a bony chest. She stared at me and said, 'Are you Grace Kelly?'

Jude burst into laughter as I smiled and shook my head. 'No, my name's Esther Chambers and I'm a private investigator. Please could you get Dennis for us?'

'Oh, OK,' she said sullenly. 'I was gonna give you a free drink if you were, that's all.'

Talkin' about my girl (my girl) . . .

Still with a smile on his face Jude nudged me and whispered, 'Esther Chambers, private investigator . . . wow . . . were you ever born to it.'

The girl gave a great shout of 'Dennis!' and the man serving behind the bar on the night of Julie's disappearance came out from the back. He was wiping his hands on a tea towel and narrowed his eyes when he saw me and Jude. He wore jeans and a green T-shirt that strained over his pot belly. The snake slithered menacingly around and around his thick arm.

'These two here want a word with

you,' said the girl, nodding in our direction before slowly going to serve a customer who was shaking an empty pint glass in her direction.

Dennis leaned towards us and said curtly, giving an upward nod, 'Can I 'elp?'

'Yeah, hopefully you can,' said Jude and went on to ask about the man with the dark ponytail.

Suddenly with a blast of brass, Shirley Bassey's voice boomed through the speakers.

Goldfinger, he's the man, the man with the Midas touch, a spider's touch . . .

'Why do you wanna know?

'A girl has gone missing,' said Jude. 'Julie Foster. She was last seen here in this bar . . . sitting right here.' He pointed to a bar stool.

'Are you the police or something?'

'No,' said Jude flashing his card. 'Jude Dunbar, private investigator. What do you know of the man with the ponytail?'

He shrugged. 'Nothing much, he just drinks in here.' His gaze shifted to me. 'I remember you, though. Pretty hard not to remember you . . .' His eyes were red-rimmed, not the clear blue of Jude's but cloudy, and ominous somehow.

'You do? Well, in that case you must remember the missing girl. She was sitting with the guy with the ponytail.' I pointed across the room. 'She was standing over there with me for a while, and then she joined the ponytail guy. She was wearing a red cat suit and,' I pointed to my neck, 'a black chiffon scarf tied with a bow, here.'

. . . such a gold finger, beckons you to enter his web of sin, but don't go in . . .

'Yeah . . . she left with the guy you're on about. I don't know who he is.'

'You're quite sure she left with that guy?'

Dennis nodded.

'Have you seen him before?' asked Jude. 'Is he a regular, maybe?'

'Yeah, but I don't know his name.'

'What's your name?'

'Dennis.'

'Your surname,' said Jude gruffly, eyeing the fella as if he was wasting his time.

He hesitated. 'Simpson . . . Dennis Simpson.'

I jotted it down.

'What's the guy's habit? Is he more likely to come in on an evening than daytime?'

'Yeah, I suppose.' Dennis shrugged again and twisted his lips as if he really didn't care.

'OK, we'll come back later.'

A group of people came clamouring around the bar, talking loudly and almost drowning out the music. The girl was still serving slowly at the other end so it looked as if this was Dennis's job.

Pretty girl, beware of his heart of gold, this heart is cold . . . this heart is cold . . .

'Hmm, seems you don't know much at the moment,' said Jude with a grin. 'Maybe you can try racking those brains for later. See ya, Dennis.'

'Whaddya want?' we heard Dennis say to the clamouring group as Jude and I tapped down the stone steps and went out into the cold, fresh air. Taking a deep breath, I smiled, looking around at the bustling streets, buses and cars shooting up and down the road. Music could still be heard faintly from Milly's. My ears were ringing as if bells had somehow got inside them.

'Come on,' said Jude, taking my hand. 'We'll go to your shop, see if Julie's turned up before we do anything else.' His eyes shone bright blue in the sunshine.

Tying my scarf firmly under my chin and putting on warm gloves, I put my hand into his. He gripped it firmly as we walked.

5

Esther baby, if you've taken up private investigating with that Paul Newman lookalike then good for you. I envy you, really I do, and hope there'll be wedding bells soon, but don't you worry about me. Martha Engleson ain't never been out of work. A friend of mine, Mrs Brodie my neighbour, she lives in the apartment next door, told me they're looking for dressers in London Girl. I'll bet you one full English pound I'll be starting my new job there before you can say hoot.'

'Mrs Rodgers said she wants you back, Martha — but looking after Jane this time instead of me. And Julie too, when she turns up.'

I was standing in the hallway, at the payphone, shivering in the cold air gusting in at the open door where a young guy with muscular arms and a broad grin was delivering sweet-smelling bread to

The Milk Maid on large, cumbersome pallets. A gust of warm air from the café mingled with the cold, making my conversation with Martha just about bearable.

'*If* she turns up, you mean.' Her voice faded and I couldn't hear what she was saying.

'Are you still there? Martha?'

Her voice came loud and clear now.

'Sorry, Esther baby, I was talking to the kitten. George brought it home last night, a little ginger scrap of a thing . . . running around the printers, it was. It's scratching the sofa now and I had to tell it off.'

'Oh wow, you have a kitten?'

'Yeah — got ink in its eyes though, I been putting drops in them. It can barely see.'

'What did you say just then about Julie?'

'I just said *if* she comes back, not when!'

'Oh Martha, surely you can be more positive than that?'

'I'm sorry honey but...' her voice faded again and then she said, 'Tell Mrs Rodgers I wouldn't go back to her place if she paid me a thousand English pounds a week. I ain't working there without you, Esther baby.'

* * *

There were posters of Julie everywhere now. On lamp posts, in pubs and clubs and shops, even here right in front of me by the telephone. I stared at her as I ended my conversation with Martha, her pretty face and bright smile. If only we had a lead on where she'd gone.

I, and everybody else including her distraught parents and brother, just wanted her back safe and modelling with Jane and Pam at Attitude.

Jude and I had been back to Milly's every night for the past week and there was still no sign of the guy with the ponytail. With Dennis, the bald bar tender, still deep in an attack of amnesia, we were no further forward with our enquiries.

We were going back there tonight but for now, Jude wanted me at his offices in Leadenhall Mansions. There were reports to type up on other cases and, because I was grappling with a brand new IBM golf ball electric typewriter, the paperwork wasn't moving as fast as I wanted it to. The speed of the machine was amazing. I had to smile when Jude said to me just the day before, 'Relax, Esther, the typewriter's not going anywhere,' when I'd complained that my fingers couldn't keep up with the pace of that damn golf ball. It was a brand new model, though, and really cool. He'd obviously put a lot of time and thought into what sort of machine would be best for me to use in his employment.

Jude was talking on the phone when I arrived, his feet in smart black brogues propped up on his desk. He held a cigarette between two fingers from which smoke curled lazily above his head. The office wasn't spacious, just this one room with a small kitchen and a toilet, but it had two beautiful arched windows letting in plenty of light. One looked out onto Leadenhall Street and the other onto the cobbled street at the side, reminding me of the layout of the Attitude shop.

He looked round as I walked in, gave me a sexy wink and mouthed, 'I won't be long . . .' and then into the phone, 'OK, Mrs Leveridge, I'll get the report typed up today and sent out by first class post.'

He listened and then said, 'Yeah, well, from what I've seen so far, there could well be another woman involved. You're best to read the report before you say anything to him though, OK?'

He leaned forward and stubbed his cigarette into a blue glass ashtray that stood on his desk. He wore a dark grey suit with a white shirt and a light grey tie. Oh, how I liked a man wearing a suit . . . especially Jude Dunbar.

At the sight of him, I wanted to go right over, hang up the phone and ensconce myself firmly on his lap, my arms around his neck and my mouth on his. Instead, I shrugged off my coat and scarf and hung them both on the coat stand. Putting my bag in a desk drawer, I started to look through the files and papers that Jude had left out to help me when I typed up the reports. I was amazed at how many women had their husbands under surveillance for suspicion of an affair — and the other way round, although not quite as many.

Jude hung up the phone with a, 'Yes, Mrs Leveridge, first class post tonight, good day to you.' Then he turned to me, his blue eyes wide and bright.

'Wow, you look lovely, Esther. I like your hair that way, and that little dress too . . . ravishing.'

Cupping the back of my head with a hand and turning it this way and that, I said, 'It's a chignon à la Grace Kelly.'

'Well, it looks great . . . and you're even more beautiful than Grace Kelly.'

Feeling a slight flush to my cheeks, I changed the subject. 'I'd better do this report first then, huh?' I said, holding up the Leveridge file.

With a slight smile on his face, he prowled across the room and came to stand behind me, cupping my shoulders with his hands and bending over, nuzzling his mouth into my neck and breathing deeply. 'Hmm, you smell good too, and I like your neck on display this way...'

Delicious shivers ran down my spine but I nudged him away and said, 'You know, maybe we shouldn't work together. It's too distracting.'

He stood up and went to sit on the edge of his desk.

'Now don't you be running off back to your modelling. We said six months, remember?'

I nodded and he said, 'What's your perfume?'

'Youth Dew.'

He reached for his packet of cigarettes and shook one out, putting it between his lips and letting it hang there for a second while he rummaged in his pocket for his lighter. He took a deep drag and said, 'Ah yeah, I thought it smelled familiar. I'll draw up a contract for you to sign — that way I'll know that I won't lose you too soon.'

I smiled, even though a little dart of jealousy shot through me at his comment about the perfume. Had he smelled it on someone else before? If so, who? His ex-wife? I didn't like to ask. Putting it to the back of my mind, I began on the reports, inserting a fresh sheet of paper into the typewriter. Beginning my battle with the dreaded golf ball, I began to type.

* * *

'Have we struck lucky tonight?' asked Jude as a man with long, black hair tied in a ponytail came lumbering along the street. Lumbering was the only word I could use because he was a big guy, tall, well over six feet, and broad in the shoulders with a flat, chiselled, sharp-featured face and deep-set eyes.

It was a cold frosty night again, verging on snow and a tiny sliver of moon hung in a navy blue sky. There weren't many people about, just one or two groups, all dressed up and going into the pubs and clubs ranged along the street, a few couples walking hand in hand. Maybe it was simply too chilly tonight and people were staying in.

He was coming closer and closer to where we were sitting in Jude's car, parked just along the road from Milly's nightclub. His skin was swarthy and his hair very black, just as I remembered.

'Esther? Is that him?'

'I think so,' I said, sitting forward in the passenger seat, and staring hard through the windscreen. It was dark now, though, and I hadn't realised how tall he was because I'd only seen him sitting down on a bar stool next to Julie.

There was a flash of gold as the man lifted a hand to his face, and suddenly I was quite sure.

'Yeah, it's him. I remember those big gold rings that he's wearing.'

'Go then, I'll wait here. Use that lovely

charm of yours. We need to speak to him before he goes into Milly's. We don't want anyone tipping him off, do we?'

'You mean Dennis?'

Jude nodded and said, 'Be careful,' as I got out of the car. Pulling my scarf further over my hair, I approached the guy with the ponytail.

'Um, excuse me . . .'

He turned abruptly with a puzzled frown, although his expression smoothed out when he saw me.

'Hey — hi there, doll. Do you want me?'

He pointed a finger at his own chest as if shocked that I would deign to speak to him. His voice was very deep and almost musical, just as you'd imagine Nat 'King' Cole or Johnny Mathis would speak.

'Yes,' I said, gathering confidence. 'I think you might be able to help me.'

'Fire away, doll . . .' He stopped and, peering closer at me, said, 'You sure look like that actress, um, what's her name? . . . hey, hey, wait a minute.' He put out a hand, palm up. 'You're not from that *Candid Camera* programme on the telly, are you?'

'No, of course not!' I took a deep breath, a bit afraid of what reaction I might get, although he seemed to be a friendly guy. 'I'm a friend of Julie Foster, the girl who's gone missing . . .'

'Oh, her, yeah, I saw a poster with her picture on earlier. Do you know, she looks just like a girl that came to chat with me in Milly's only about a week ago . . .'

'Really?' I said, nodding at Jude who I knew was watching me, ready for the signal to get out of the car and come forward. 'You know her, then?'

'Not until last week, no. She just came and sat with me at the bar . . . wanted a couple of free drinks, I thought at the time. That's if it is her?'

I knew that was true because I'd witnessed it with my own eyes.

'Yes, it was her — Julie Foster, that is — who you were talking to. I know because I saw you with her.'

He looked puzzled and then caught sight of Jude.

'Hey, who are you?'

Jude wore his Fedora hat and his long tan coat, the collar pulled up high around his neck and ears.

'Jude Dunbar, private investigator,' he said flashing a card. 'There's no need for alarm, we're carrying out investigations into the disappearance of Julie Foster.'

'I'm his assistant, Esther Chambers,' I told him. 'We've been looking out for you every night for over a week.'

'Yeah, I been working away — every other week, truck driving, a firm called Eddie's.' He went on, 'I wouldn't harm a hair on that girl's head. In fact, I wouldn't harm a hair on nobody's head.'

'We're not saying that you have or you would. Is there anywhere we can talk? It's cold out here.'

I was shivering, my lips numb and probably blue too, and my heart rose when Jude said that. A private investigator needed to either wear thicker clothes or more clothes than a model ever had to, that's for sure.

'Milly's?' asked the guy.

'No — somewhere else,' replied Jude. 'We've spoken to the bartender in there and he's not very friendly.'

The guy started to laugh. 'Who, Dennis?'

'The guy with the bald head and snake tattoo?'

'Yeah, that's him. I know a little place around the corner, Leopold's. Fancy one in there?'

We both nodded and walked with him along the frosty pavement. A few fat snowflakes had begun to fall and I slithered a little on the icy path. Jude smiled and held my arm to steady me. He offered his cigarette packet to the guy who took one readily and stuck it behind his ear.

'For later,' he said with a wink.

The snow began to fall faster, settling on the guy's black ponytail like a bad case of dandruff.

'You know who Dennis is, though,

don't you?' he asked as we reached the entrance to the bar. The building had a black frontage with Leopold's painted across it in big gold letters. Red lamps shone out of the windows giving a rosy glow and I could see people sitting inside, drinking and talking at tables littered with glasses and bottles.

We both shook our heads, and then Jude said in what seemed a serious tone, 'The London Ripper?' He gave himself away with a chuckle.

'No . . . good guess, though.' The guy grinned. 'He's the stolen baby.' And when we both still looked puzzled, he leaned in close and said, 'He was stolen from his pram when he was a baby. Did you never read about in the papers or hear about it?'

We both shook our heads and he said, 'Yeah, maybe a bit before your time. Me and Dennis are probably at least twenty years older than you two. I grew up knowing about it as a kid. My mum used to threaten to have us kidnapped like Dennis Simpson if we played up. I couldn't believe it was him when I started drinking in Milly's.'

'Dennis said that he didn't know your name,' I told him.

'He knows my name alright . . . everyone in Milly's does. I'm Marty Valesko.' He gave a little mock bow. 'Pleased to meet you!'

After the cold outside, the heat hit us hard as we walked into the bar.

* * *

I awoke the next day, my eyes heavy and my head feeling like a twenty-pound weight on the pillow. I wasn't sure I'd be able to lift it, and thought I might have to stay here forever like a modern-day Sleeping Beauty.

Vague memories of the night before echoed through my mind, particularly Jude's heavenly blue eyes looking into mine as I sipped at a sparkly drink called Babycham, served in a wide glass on a stem embossed with a cute little Bambi figure, a couple of cherries on a stick swirling amongst the bubbles. A private investigator's life wasn't for the faint-hearted, that's for sure.

Stumbling out of bed, I went into the kitchen for two headache pills that I washed down with a glass of water. Marty Valesko had introduced me to the Babycham, that seemingly innocent little drink, sweet and fizzy as Coca-Cola, so I blamed him for how I was feeling this morning.

Glancing at my bright orange kitchen clock, I realised I had to hurry if I was going to be on time to meet Jude at the library — for some research, as he called it.

Although last night Marty Valesko had filled us in on information about Dennis Simpson the bartender, we still didn't have a clue where Julie could be and she'd been gone for over a week now. I was worried — afraid that time was running out for her.

'Did you see her home?' I remembered Jude asking Marty as we sat in the cosy bar the previous night. A real open fire was curling its way, bright orange and red, up the chimney and tiny hot sparks were spitting at the fireguard like an angry snake.

'No way, man,' said Marty Valesko. 'I went to the gents and when I got back, she was gone.'

He took a sip from his pint of beer. He looked cool and casual wearing a pair of blue jeans and a black polo necked jumper, a black leather jacket open over the top. The gold rings flashed as he picked up his glass and took a deep draught.

'How about Dennis? Was he gone, too?'

A group of people at the table next to ours suddenly let out a great bellow of laughter, making me jump, and the juke box began to play.

Sugar pie honey bunch, you know that I love you, I can't help myself... Jude discreetly stretched out a hand and squeezed mine tightly. I squeezed his back... *I love you and nobody else.*

'I didn't see him, but everything was

being closed up for the night anyway, it was late.' He flushed shyly as he said, 'I wanted to ask Julie for a number where I could contact her. But, as I said, she was gone. A bit out of my league anyway, I would think.'

He took the cigarette that Jude had given him from behind his ear and put it between his lips. Jude lit it for him and took one for himself too, taking a deep drag, and turning his head away from me as he blew out the smoke in a long grey funnel.

'Dennis told us that Julie left Milly's with you.'

'No — she didn't leave with me. That's a lie.'

'Do you remember me?' I asked him. 'I was standing with Julie when she said she'd seen a cute guy and would I mind if she went to talk to him.'

'She really said that?' he asked, flushing again. 'Wow...' And then, 'Yeah, I remember you ... only because Dennis pointed you out, though.'

Jude and I exchanged glances and a

shiver ran up my spine.

'What did he say?' I asked.

'Something like, 'Wow, have you seen her? Classy!' Or maybe it was 'what a doll' . . . something along those lines.'

I felt a slight chill at a man twenty years older saying something like that about me.

'So, what you were saying about Dennis? He was a stolen baby?'

Sugar pie honey bunch, I'm weaker than a man should be . . .

'Yeah, taken from his pram that was in his own back yard.'

'Was he found and taken back to his parents?'

'No, apparently he tried to contact them a couple of years ago but both his mum and dad had died so it was too late. It affected him badly — said he didn't know who he really was. Stuff like that, you know?'

'Who told him he'd been snatched? How did he know he had other parents?'

'The woman who he thought was his mum told him on her deathbed, a full confession. She even told him to contact his real parents — told him she was sorry, all that baloney.'

'What about the man he thought was his dad?'

'Nah, he'd died long before.'

I dragged my mind back to the present. Glancing at my little Ingersoll watch I noticed the time and rushed into the bathroom, turning on the taps for a bath and then into the bedroom, searching for another pair of tights. Two pairs of tights under my miniskirt, although not incredibly sexy, should keep me warmer than I'd been yesterday.

What Dennis Simpson being stolen from his pram as a baby had to do with Julie, I wasn't sure, but Jude said he had a feeling that we should look into it. Thoughts of Julie the last time I saw her, looking so beautiful in her red cat suit and chiffon scarf bow, sped through my mind as I got dried and dressed and let myself out of the flat, almost running all the way to the library in my haste to meet Jude.

6

The library was hushed as I pushed my way through the revolving doors and into the massive entrance area. Long bars of sunlight fell through the tall windows set high up on the walls, pooling on the forest green carpet like lozenges of gold dust.

There were hundreds of wooden shelving units stocked full of books in every genre imaginable. Large signs hung above each unit, *Historical*, *Comedy*, *Action and Adventure*, *Crime*, *Horror*. Jude was talking to the librarian, asking her where we could find archive newspapers.

We followed her broad figure into an adjoining room, furnished with a couple of tables and some chairs, boxes and boxes of newspapers piled up on shelves. It was good to see that the room was empty and that Jude and I would be alone to do our research.

'You're better to use the microfiche,' the librarian told us. 'It's really easy to use and some of the newspapers could fall to dust if you handle them. I'm not saying you can't look at them, but please be careful.' She showed us how to use the machine and then said, 'Well, I'll leave you to it, is that all right?'

We nodded and thanked her and she bustled off quickly to deal with a queue of people that had suddenly formed at the enquiries desk.

'Now then,' I said, all professionalism and business. 'I'm going to have a look through these newspapers here.' I pulled out a box labelled *1921-25*. If Dennis Simpson was twenty years older than me, he must have been born around 1923. 'You can start off looking at the microfiche if you like . . .'

'Hey,' said Jude. 'Not so fast, Esther baby.' He pulled me into his arms.

'Not here in the library!' I whispered. 'Someone might see us.'

'There's no one here,' he whispered, his breath tickling my ear, making me squirm and giggle. 'Mm, you smell nice . . . Youth Dew again?'

I nodded, tempted to ask where he'd smelled it before, but put it on the back burner for now. At the moment finding Julie was more important.

Jude started waltzing me around, his dance moves surprisingly smooth and elegant.

'*Oh Esther baby*,' he crooned, '*I'm in the mood for love, simply because you're near me, I'm in the mood for love . . .*'

'Jude!'

'*I'm in the mood for love . . .*' and then he said, 'Marry me?'

I stopped dead still, pulling away from him, looking at his face. 'Are you serious?'

'I sure am. *I'm in the mood for love* . . . simply because . . .' He hummed the tune and held out his arms.

My heart soared and then sank again, conflicting feelings fighting inside me.

'We hardly know each other, Jude. You're being silly.'

'Well, if that's how you're going to

treat my marriage proposal . . .' he said lightly.

I shook my head at him, still not sure if he was serious.

'Fine,' I said carelessly. 'Ask me again in a few months' time.'

'OK.' He nodded, looking at me from the corner of his baby blues. 'I will, you know. I will ask you again.' Suddenly, he pulled me close and kissed my mouth hard.

'Really!' hissed a voice. We looked round. The librarian stood in the doorway, a finger to her lips. 'Silence in the library . . . please . . .' She walked away, her whole stance disgruntled.

We exchanged mischievous glances as I went to retrieve the newspapers from the box. Jude, still quietly humming the same tune, started to do battle with the microfiche machine.

* * *

We worked quietly and steadily, it seemed for hours. Eventually Jude whispered, 'Esther, I've gotta nip outside.' He brandished his walkie talkie. 'I have to check in with the police every few days, tell them what we're doing. Will you be OK here?'

'Of course.'

'If you haven't found anything by the time I get back, we'll go grab something to eat, OK?'

I nodded and smiled as he leaned over and kissed my cheek, giving me a sexy wink. I watched him as he walked away, his stride long and easy, before turning back to the newspapers, puzzled as to why I hadn't found anything throughout 1923 about the stolen baby.

A sudden thought came to me and, annoyed that I hadn't thought of it before, I turned to look through the newspapers for 1924. If Dennis Simpson hadn't been born until the end of 1923, he wouldn't have been snatched until early the following year. That's if he had been born in 1923 at all. What a hopeless task — and more than likely not anything to do with Julie going missing at all. Maybe we were wasting our time.

Laboriously I turned the pages, licking my ink-stained fingers to get a purchase on the paper, trying to be careful as the Librarian had told us to be. Suddenly a front page headline screamed out at me, *Baby Stolen From Pram In Broad Daylight!*

At last! I began to read the tiny print, straining my eyes, and in the end, standing up and going to the window where bright light shone through, so I could see more clearly. Avidly I read the article, frowning as I realised that this must be about a different baby. The name wasn't right; this wasn't Dennis Simpson. In fact, there was no mention of the name Simpson.

The article showed a black and white picture of a baby sleeping in a beautiful Silver Cross pram, one of the best you could get. There was a grainy picture of the baby's parents, a young couple, sitting outside on striped deckchairs, their hands loosely threaded together. It must have been before the event for they looked happy and relaxed, smiling for the camera. Something about the two of them looked familiar, and I felt sure I'd seen this picture before.

With my heart thumping almost into my ears, our old red album came to mind, and I could see Dad sitting at the table proudly inserting photos into its blank pages. Mostly me, at every milestone of my life, some of Mum and Dad when they were young and courting.

Suddenly, the name *Fishbourne* jumped out at me from the tiny print beneath the picture.

'*Mr and Mrs Fishbourne whose only son, Dennis, was stolen from his pram yesterday.*'

In shock, I let the newspaper slip from my hands. It fluttered to the floor, coming to rest softly on the green carpet like a great black and white butterfly.

Hands cupping my mouth, I stood, shaking, until Jude came back. After picking up the newspaper and scanning the article, he laid it carefully on the table, then took me into his arms and drew me close without a word.

* * *

'Drink this,' said Jude, thrusting a squat glass, containing maybe an inch of dark liquid, into my hand. The smell was pungent and it slid down my throat like a liquid flame. 'It'll stop you shaking.'

Music was playing. *I just don't know what to do with myself, don't know just what to do with myself . . .*

'What is it?' I croaked, hardly able to speak. My throat felt as if it would burst into flames.

He took off his hat and put it on the table revealing his hair, thick and red-gold and springing back from his forehead. His wispy moustache had gone, replaced by a sexy stubble.

'Brandy.' He knocked back his own with a flick of the wrist. 'I've got some food coming, too.'

'I can't eat, Jude.'

Going to the movies only makes me sad,

parties make me feel as bad . . .

'Yes, you can.'

We were in Leopold's again, sitting close to where we'd sat last night, the fire still blazing and spitting embers onto the fireguard. It was lunchtime and fairly busy with business men in suits and women wearing smart clothes who I took to be secretaries or assistants like me.

I peeled off my gloves and opened my coat, loosened my scarf and rested my head against the wall behind me. Jude leaned forward and gently took my hand.

'Are you OK, Esther?' he asked in concern.

'I don't know,' I said, close to tears again. 'Why didn't they tell me? All those years and they didn't say a word. People must have known, yet nobody told me.'

Jude shook his head sadly.

'Look, think about it. You were only eighteen when they died. Maybe they were going to tell you but were waiting, say, until you were twenty-one.'

Come back, I will be around, just waiting for you . . . I don't know what else to do.

I nodded and sniffed.

'You could be right. They were awfully old-fashioned, you know . . .' I felt another deep pang of guilt at the thought of them.

'And maybe they felt as if there was a sort of stigma about it all. That they didn't protect their baby from being taken. Do you see what I mean?'

I nodded, agreeing with him, just as there was a great shout from the bar. Jude jumped up and came back carrying two portions of chicken and chips in the basket closely followed by a barman carrying knives and forks, red and brown sauce, salt and pepper.

Brandishing his knife, Jude said, 'Eat, Esther . . . it'll do you good.'

Reluctantly I speared a chip with my fork and chewed it listlessly. Jude nodded.

'That's good — come on, eat up. Do you want salt? Pepper?'

'Hmm, maybe pepper, thank you.'

Handing it to me, he said, 'You should always have pepper with you, Esther.'

Sprinkling it liberally, I said, 'Why?'

'I have a little story for you. I once had a cheating husband confront me in a bar. With a little help from me, his wife had found out about his other woman and he wasn't happy. He wanted to take it out on me. I tried to defend myself, and he threw pepper in my eyes. Ow . . . Esther, it really hurt.'

'Oh my God,' I said in horror.

'All I'm saying is, if you ever do need to defend yourself against someone, throw pepper at them . . . go for the eyes.' He smiled and took a bite from a chip. 'Anyway, let's get back to Marty Valesko.'

'Yeah, I won't forget that useful trick,' I said. 'So, do you think Marty's telling the truth? If he is, it could be that Dennis Simpson is my brother! Well, actually he'd be Dennis Fishbourne . . . no wonder he changed his name!'

'Yeah, I do . . . and yeah.' He laughed and raised his eyebrows. 'You look nothing alike. And do you know what?'

I looked at him enquiringly.

'I think he has Julie.'

Like a summer rose, it needs the sun and rain . . .

'Oh, Jude.' I cut up a piece of chicken and put it in my mouth, shaking my head.

'Yeah, to get to you . . . I have a hunch.' He was thinking, his lovely blue eyes, unfocussed and far away. 'He knows who you are. We need to pay him another visit, Esther. Prepare yourself for tomorrow.'

'Tomorrow?' I asked him. 'Why not today?'

I ate some more chicken and nibbled on another chip. The food was making me feel stronger, more resolute and unafraid, and I suppose the brandy had helped with that as well.

'I've got to put my personal feelings aside for the time being and concentrate on the job we're doing, which is looking for Julie. It was just such a shock to see their picture like that, in the newspaper.'

Wiping his mouth on a napkin, Jude took a cigarette from the packet and held it between two fingers before putting it to his mouth and striking his lighter.

'You're a brave woman, Esther,' he said, and then, nodding at my almost empty basket, 'I told you you'd be able to eat.'

'You were right, it's made me feel better. Look, all I want is for Dennis Simpson to tell me the truth, and for Julie to be back, safe...'

He took a deep drag on his cigarette and patted my hand.

'Don't worry, Esther, we'll get her back.'

* * *

Milly's was just the same as it had been a few days before. It was filled with the usual suspects; men drinking alone or in groups, pints of beer or packs of cards on the tables. The place stank of stale perfume and beer, and the music was still excruciatingly loud, the Stones bellowing out their latest hit.

I can't get no satisfaction . . . cause I try,

and I try and I try . . .

The girl who'd been working before was there, slowly serving at the other end of the bar, her face sullen and her neckline low. There was no sign of Dennis Simpson.

A young man, all Robert Redford blond hair and Californian good looks, came over to serve us. He was smartly dressed in black trousers and a shirt swirling with bright flowers and leaves.

'Hey guys, what can I get you?'

He had a blue and white tea towel draped over one shoulder and looked ready for action. Totally out of place in this down-at-heel bar.

I can't get no . . . satisfaction . . .

Jude flashed his card. 'Jude Dunbar, private investigator and my assistant, Esther Chambers.' He nodded towards me and then looked back at the young man. 'Is Dennis Simpson around?'

'No,' he said, looking slightly afraid — at the words *private investigator*, I suppose. 'He ain't been in for a few days.'

'Is he sick?'

'I don't know. I'm just standing in until he comes back.'

'Have you got an address for him?' I asked.

. . . hey hey hey . . . that's what I say . . .

'No, ma'am.' He was staring at me as if I was some sort of apparition. I was sure he was going to ask the dreaded question: *Are you Grace Kelly*? But all he said was, 'I can't give out that sort of information, sorry.'

I noticed that the girl, still serving at the other end of the bar, had one beady eye on us and one on her very patient customers.

'Are you sure you haven't got that information?' asked Jude, giving him the dead eye.

Pulling himself up to his full height, the barman stammered, 'No sir, sorry sir, but I haven't . . . sir.'

Jude nodded and said, 'OK, we'll be back tomorrow . . . and every day until we can speak to Dennis Simpson. Do you understand?'

Swallowing hard and nodding, the young guy said, 'Yes sir, I understand, sir.'

'What's your name?' asked Jude.

'Mike Fromer, sir.'

'OK then, Mike, we'll see you tomorrow.'

'Yes sir, ma'am,' he said as we walked away.

Outside in the cold fresh air, among the people milling about on the street, Jude smiled wryly and shook his head as he tipped a cigarette out of an almost full packet and lit it.

'You put the fear of God into that poor young man,' I observed.

'Yeah, I know. He's a good guy, he stood by his guns. Too good for that place.' He took a deep drag and blew the smoke away from me.

'What do we do now?' I asked him.

'Wait until tomorrow,' he said, his tone disappointed and flat.

I felt let down and frustrated, the newspaper article and Julie in the forefront of my mind.

I felt a tap on my shoulder and a voice said, 'You looking for Dennis again, then?'

We turned to see the girl from the bar. She looked older than in the dim lighting of Milly's, deep wrinkles etched around her eyes and mouth. She was shivering, skinny arms crossed over her bony chest.

'I know where he lives,' she told us. 'For a price.'

'What sort of price?' asked Jude.

'Cigarettes?'

'Here.' He thrust the almost full packet at her. 'Now tell us where he lives.'

'It's not even full,' she complained, peering into the package, mouth down turned.

'I'll get you more,' he replied. 'Now, tell us . . .'

'Norfolk Terrace.' Eagerly she took a cigarette from the packet and put it in her mouth. Jude lit it for her. A red double decker bus trundled past and the conductor, hanging on at the back, smiled at me and gave a cheeky wave.

'Number ten, I think . . . and don't tell anyone I told you.'

Jude thanked her and she scurried back inside, taking deep drags of the cigarette as if her life depended on it. My heart racing, I glanced at Jude. His blue eyes glowed in a strong shaft of sunlight.

'I can't believe it, but that's where I grew up,' I told him. 'Ten, Norfolk Terrace. Mum and Dad always lived there. That's where Dennis Simpson will have been taken from as a baby.'

'Come on, Esther, let's go,' he said, throwing his glowing cigarette stub onto the pavement and grinding it out with his shoe. 'Let's go find Julie.'

7

You missed him by about ten minutes,' said a voice. We'd just arrived at number ten, Norfolk Terrace, a tall row of Victorian houses, and were rat-tat-tatting with the door knocker.

A brass lion's head, it used to be so shiny, polished by Mum every day. Now it was dull and tarnished. The door was dusty and could do with a coat of paint.

We knocked again hoping, but not really expecting, that Dennis Simpson would open the door so that we could see the expression on his face when we asked him about Julie.

Why he'd decided to live in this house was a mystery to me. Was it because he'd been deprived of a life he could have had here? If that was the case, it made me wonder what sort of parents his kidnappers had been.

I'd inherited the house. Both Mum and Dad had been sticklers for having an up-to-date will and, after clearing everything out, I'd sold it to a young couple with two little kids. I didn't want to stay there all alone.

I'd had no idea that they'd moved out and he'd moved in. Up until the night I went into Milly's, I'd never seen Dennis Simpson before.

We'd been outside for ages and, even with two pairs of tights underneath my skirt, I was freezing in the cold March wind. Wasn't it supposed to get warmer when the daffodils are blooming?

We'd come in Jude's car, which he'd parked on the street next to this one. When I'd asked why, he said, 'It's best to be cautious, Esther. If he's at home, it might scare him off if he sees a car he doesn't recognise parking outside.'

The voice rang out again. 'You've missed him, love. He's not in.'

It belonged to the next door neighbour, a small woman with curly, dark hair and an anxious smile, who peered over the dilapidated fence between the two houses. She wore a wraparound flowered pinny, which not only reminded me of Martha but my mum too, giving me a pang as if I'd gone back in time. I didn't recognise her, so assumed that the elderly Mr and Mrs Lewis who lived there before I left home, had moved away or maybe even died and she was the new owner.

'Oh — OK, thanks,' said Jude.

'I'm surprised you didn't bump into him,' she said. 'He's been gone literally ten minutes. Anything I might be able to help you with, like?'

'No, no, it's fine, thank you,' Jude said and we walked down the path and back onto the street.

'Well-meaning or just plain nosey,' he said quietly, and then, 'Our luck's in, Esther. He's not here — we'll have to break in.'

I giggled and whispered, 'Yes, we can try round the back . . .'

Jude nodded as we tip-tapped around the back of the houses onto a cobbled street littered with the inevitable big silver bins and rubbish skittering about, blown by the breeze. The area had certainly gone downhill since I'd lived here. My mum and dad would never have stood for rubbish flying about in the back alley.

We found number ten's back garden, which had a couple of big flower planters standing on the flagstones. They were falling to pieces, the wood crumbling, the flowers brown and dead. Looking around, it was hard to believe this was the place where I used to play with all the local kids with balls and skipping ropes, dolls and dressing-up clothes.

Jude climbed the three little steps to the back door and pushed down on the handle, looking not at all surprised that it was locked. Stepping back down, we looked up at all the windows, all closed.

'I'll have to break the door down,' he said. 'Stand back.'

'Hey, wait a minute,' I said, 'I've got an idea . . .' I reached under the threadbare brown mat on the top step and, with a big smile on my face, drew out a long silver key.

‘Well, whaddya know,’ said Jude quietly, stifling laughter as I inserted the key into the lock and opened the door. ‘Esther Chambers, private investigator extraordinaire!’

‘We always left the key there,’ I told him. ‘Nothing changes and everything does, eh?’

‘Well, Dennis Simpson obviously doesn’t think we suspect him for one second . . . or, hang on, do you think he left the key on purpose?’

We walked straight into the kitchen, which was virtually empty except for a small red-topped Formica table and four chairs. A wooden dresser along one wall was coated with dust. It smelled stale and tired as if no one had cooked in there for a very long time. So different to the kitchen I’d known. The hallway looked virtually the same, except that the carpet had gone and a length of brown sticky-looking lino covered the floor. Dogeared leaflets and envelopes were scattered all over the door mat.

‘Wow, what a change in a house,’ I

said softly, thinking of what it had been like when I was a child and growing up.

Jude shook his head sadly.

'Yeah, I can imagine.'

I peered around the sitting room door, half afraid that Dennis Simpson would be sitting there waiting for us, a shotgun or a knife in his hand, but apart from a threadbare sofa, two chairs and a television, the room was empty. My imagination seemed to be getting the better of me.

'Oh God, Jude, what if she's not here?'

I suddenly felt so afraid that she wouldn't be, that the trail was cold and we'd never see her again.

'Ssh,' he said, grabbing my hand as we cautiously started to climb the stairs, one step at a time, tiptoeing quietly, for the steps were bare of any carpet as well.

'Julie?' said Jude suddenly. 'Julie?'

There was a rustling from somewhere and a banging as if something had been dropped.

Three doors stood open, two of the bedrooms and the bathroom, their shabby contents visible from the landing. The other door was closed.

I went right up to it and said, my forehead against the cold hard wood, 'Julie?'

There was a squeaking sound as if mice were in there. I tried the handle but it was locked.

'Stand clear, Esther,' Jude said. He ran forward and rammed his shoulder into the door once, twice and on the third try, the door swung open.

There was a flash of red and a mewling sound as a figure tried to sit up, her hair thin rats' tails now and her pretty black chiffon scarf a gag in her mouth.

'Julie!' Rushing to her, I pulled down the gag and she collapsed against me crying weakly.

'Oh Esther, Esther . . . thank God you're here . . . thank God.'

I hugged her tight, her body feeling even lighter and bonier than ever before.

'Did he hurt you?' I asked.

Tears in her eyes, she shook her head.

I heard Jude talking on his walkie talkie before he came and hunkered down beside us, his face grave. He rubbed Julie's bare shoulder saying, 'It's OK now, Julie, it's OK...' as we fumbled with the green garden twine Dennis Simpson had used to tie her wrists together.

* * *

Still reeling with all that had happened over the past few days and relieved that Julie was safe and well, and finally at home — although she'd moved back in with her parents for a while — I'd come into the office to get some reports typed up for Jude.

He'd gone to see a new case. A woman searching for her sister, who had been adopted before she was born. She was desperate to contact her, had tried adoption agencies to no avail, and had, apparently, become quite emotional when speaking to Jude on the telephone.

'Another interesting case I can really get my teeth into,' he'd said with a grin as we'd kissed lingeringly when we'd parted the evening before.

'Now, don't go into the office tomorrow,' he'd told me. 'Dennis Simpson hasn't turned up either at work or home. The police are looking for him, so the onus is on them now to keep you safe — and Julie too. After what we saw on the walls of Julie's prison, we don't want to take any chances. The police have been informed of the connection between you and Dennis.'

I'd nodded and told him no way would I go to the office.

For that reason he'd go mad if he knew I was here now, and I felt a stab of guilt at the lie I'd told him. My mind went back over what had been on the walls of the room that Julie had been kept in.

They were literally covered with random photos of me . . . walking to work, sitting in the park, talking to Jude, and most worrying of all, pictures of me going in and out of The Milk Maid, so it was obvious that he knew where I lived and who I was working with. It seemed that from the moment he had found out about his real parents and about me, he had been my stalker. And I hadn't even known it.

Peering from the window, I saw that it was raining, big fat drops that plopped onto the pavement and burst with a little splat, like a tiny polythene bag full of water.

I was half way through the last report, but I had a sudden urge to go and see the girls at Attitude. I was sure they'd be pleased to see me — except for Pam, of course, but that didn't bother me one bit. Now that I was winning my battle with the golf ball typewriter, my work was getting done faster, so I knew I could finish the report easily tomorrow morning.

Taking my coat from the stand, I shrugged it on and, pulling a scarf over my head, left the office, locking the door behind me.

Gazing carefully around when I got outside just in case Derek Simpson was lurking nearby, I ducked my head down, holding my collar up tight around my neck and began the short walk to the shop. I noticed a nondescript car parked at the kerb and assumed it was my protectors, the police. It was still raining but not so hard now, a light drizzle like long silver needles floating through the air. The sky was dull and there was no discernible cloud, just endless grey.

Several newspapers were on display outside the newsagent as I passed, their headlines screaming, *Missing Girl Julie Foster Safe And At Home! Missing Girl Reunited With Family*, or *Missing Girl Found All In One Piece*. I found that one in pretty poor taste.

Thoughts ran through my mind as I hurried along, splashing through puddles in my knee-high boots. The reason Dennis Simpson kidnapped Julie was still beyond my comprehension. After all if he was my stalker, why didn't he take me?

Maybe it had been a dummy run and I would be next. After all, what sort of a kidnapping was it? He hadn't asked for money for her release; she was unharmed (thank God); and he'd gone out, leaving her alone in the house with the key under the mat.

A shiver ran down my spine at the thought of being taken by him, but then all of a sudden, like a light bulb coming on, I knew what he wanted.

It was so simple. Why hadn't I realised it before? He wanted his inheritance — the money from the sale of Mum and Dad's house, or at least some of it, even though he lived in the house now anyway. In which case, why did he want the money? Unless he wanted it for somebody else. But who? Maybe that wasn't the reason. I felt upset and confused.

I had an urge to speak to Jude but had no idea where he was, apart from seeing a new client. A telephone box came into view so I ducked inside to give his flat number a try but it rang and rang. There was no point in trying the office; I knew he wasn't there. I'd have to wait until later, when we'd arranged to meet in The Milk Maid for coffee.

I'd made the decision, though, that in order to get Dennis Simpson off my back he could have what he wanted. I still had the money, invested in stocks and shares and savings accounts. He could have it all! I didn't care.

* * *

Arriving at Attitude I let myself in at the back entrance and ran up the stairs, pulling off my scarf and shaking out the raindrops. Peering around the dressing room door, I saw Pam and Jane sitting in front of the mirror fixing their faces, ready for the next onslaught of customers.

Jane jumped up when she saw me and, flung her arms around my neck.

'Esther! Oh wow, it's so good to see you.'

The room smelled of make-up and powder and some sweet perfume.

Pam's response was of course vastly different.

'What do you think you're doing here,

Esther baby?' she drawled with great sarcasm. 'If Mrs Rodgers sees you, she'll kick your sorry backside, that's for sure.'

She stood there, her hands on her hips, head thrust forward on her shoulders. Her beautiful auburn hair hung loose around her usually pretty face which looked mean and distorted by her foul mood.

'I've no argument with Mrs Rodgers,' I told her. 'Everything's cool between us now. We had a talk.'

Mrs Rodgers had apologised to me privately on the phone for calling me a thief, while asking me to go back to Attitude.

'Not any more,' Pam said through gritted teeth. 'Everybody knows that Julie was taken because of you.'

'Hey, that's not true,' protested Jane. 'This has nothing to do with Esther.'

'The kidnapper knows her,' Pam replied, glaring at Jane. 'It's all her fault.' She pointed an accusing finger at me but I stood calm.

'Jude and I found her, Pam. If we

hadn't gone snooping around, she'd still be there now . . . or worse . . . and before all this, I had no idea who the kidnapper was. It was all news to me.'

None of us heard the squeak of the door as it opened but we all turned when we heard a voice.

'That's all true. Esther and Jude found me. God knows what would have happened if they hadn't.'

Julie stood in the doorway.

Jane ran over to her and they held each other tight, their arms entwined like vines, Julie saying how relieved she was to be back at work and that she just wanted to forget about her ordeal.

She wore a black maxi coat, fastened at the front with just one large button, so it swung open to reveal a short red skirt and black wet-look knee-high boots. A red chiffon scarf covered her blonde hair.

Mrs Rodgers bustled in behind her saying, 'Julie's back working now, so can all of you just make her welcome, and no more talk about whose fault the kidnapping was. It's over, OK?'

She stood glaring at us all, as skinny and tall as a flamingo in her very short skirt and white tights. She didn't seem surprised to see me.

Pam sniffed. 'Oh well, and didn't I know that Esther baby would be forgiven in all this? She's the favourite for sure.'

'Now listen here, lady,' said Mrs Rodgers, in her calm but deadly voice. 'I favour girls who come here to work and help make my business a success, and not ones who waste their time being spiteful about their work colleagues. You hear me?'

Pam flounced back to the mirror and began to paint thick black lines around her eyes, jabbing angrily with a pencil, making me fear for her sight.

'Hey, Esther,' whispered Mrs Rodgers, taking me to one side. 'Do you think Martha will come back to work here?'

I shrugged. 'I think you're too late. She rang me the other day and said she's working at London Girl now. But if she doesn't like it there, who knows?'

Yeah, Martha had added that I owed her one full English pound for the bet we'd supposedly had.

'Why did she have to follow you?' Mrs Rodgers threw up her hands in despair. 'She ain't even working with you now!'

'I know. I'm sorry, it's my fault — but I was pushed into leaving.' I gave a tiny jerk of my head towards Pam.

'Yeah, look, everything I said before still stands. If you ever wanna come back I'd bite your hand off, OK?'

'Yeah, I'll bear that in mind but at the moment I'm quite happy working with Jude . . .'

'Yeah, I don't blame you,' my former boss replied, giving me a rough nudge with her elbow. 'Who wouldn't with a man like him?' She shook her head, staring into space, mesmerised by whatever picture she could see in her mind. 'It's those eyes. You're a lucky girl.'

I gave a smile. 'The job is interesting too.'

She nudged me again and gave a short bark of laughter. 'Yeah, right . . .'

Shaking my head at Mrs Rodger's comments, I left Attitude to go and meet Jude. The rain had virtually stopped now, just light spits and spots as I dodged around the puddles.

I truly was enjoying the job; I felt as if we were doing something positive. After all, Julie had been found because of us. I'd have gone back to modelling no problem if I hadn't been happy, regardless of Jude and his good looks. After all, it was possible to have both an interesting job and an interesting man, wasn't it?

* * *

The police were still sitting in their nondescript car when I arrived at the café and, peering through the big plate glass window, I could see Jude sitting at a table, sipping coffee, his hat on the chair beside him. My heart was beating fast. Wow, even though I'd tried not to, I'd fallen hook, line and sinker.

He glanced up, saw me and raised a

hand in greeting, a smile hovering around his luscious lips. My heart thumping in anticipation, I pushed open the door, a fug of warm air hitting me hard as I walked towards him, smiling and holding out my hands.

8

Jude took a sip of steaming coffee, telling me eagerly about the new case he'd been looking into.

'She's looking for her sister,' he told me. 'Apparently her mum had a child when she was very young and was forced to give the baby up for adoption. Well, Rose, the mum, died recently and Suzanne wants to find her sister.'

The Milk Maid was busy for tea time with people enjoying their ever popular fry-ups, or sipping from drinks and staring morosely through the window at the busy street. It was warm and fuggy, with the noise of people chattering and a faint beat coming from the jukebox.

'So her mum gave up a child for adoption and then went on to have another child?'

'Yeah, Suzanne's eighteen now and the sister will be around twenty-two. So the mother must have been in a better place four years later to keep her child that time. That happens quite a lot, Esther.'

'That's really sad, Jude.' I blew on my coffee, sending little scuds of foam across the surface. The door pinged as a customer went out and someone else came in, drenched through and dripping an umbrella everywhere. Glancing out of the window I saw that it was raining hard again, little drops racing each other down the steamed-up plate glass window.

'Yeah, I know.' He snaked his hand across the table and clasped mine. 'I'd like to find her — reunite them, you know?'

'Yeah, it would be wonderful if you could.

What's her name? . . . The adopted girl, I mean.'

He fished a notebook from his pocket, where I could see his writing squiggling across the pages.

'Rose Fletcher,' he said. 'Unless, of course, the people who adopted her changed her name. That's what makes it so hard to track people down.'

'Have you any pictures of Rose, the mother, or Rose the baby — or even the sister?'

'No, she's going to dig some out for next time. Apparently her mother hated having her picture taken so there won't be many. She doesn't think there'll be any of her mother with Rose. She said that there are very few photographs in the family at all.'

'What about the father?'

'The father left her mother when she had baby Rose. He was only seventeen or eighteen. Then the mother had a relationship with someone else which didn't last — no children by the way. And then the father came back, and Rose became pregnant with Suzanne. He stayed until she was about two and then took off again. Suzanne has never met her father.'

'Wow, what a useless man!'

His eyes clouded. 'Yeah. Some men make me ashamed to be a man.'

Gently I patted his hand. 'So they would be full sisters then, the same mother and father?'

'Yep. Full sisters indeed.'

'Her mother was so young when she died, wasn't she?'

'Yeah, only thirty-eight. She went the same way as her dad, apparently — a heart attack.'

'Such a tragedy.' I raised my coffee cup to him and said, 'Well, here's hoping for a successful reconciliation. What can I do to help?'

'There are notes to be typed and a new case file set up. We'll go to the office together. I don't like you being there alone, not until Dennis Simpson's whereabouts are known.'

I watched him intently as he fished a cigarette from the packet and prepared to light up. A bad habit, but I always got a thrill from watching him smoke.

I changed the subject, not wanting to talk about the office. It was all very well telling one white lie but any more would be wrong. I told him I'd been to see the girls at Attitude.

'All is forgiven with Mrs Rodgers now, but Pam still hates my guts . . . oh, but Julie came in while I was there. She stood up for me against Pam's bullying, and Jane did as well.'

'Pam doesn't hate your guts,' Jude said easily. 'She's jealous, that's all. Of your looks, and your popularity with the customers.'

'Pam's pretty too, and has her own share of customers,' I objected.

'Not in your league though, Esther baby. You're stylish, classy...'

'And you're just biased,' I said, leaning forward and giving him a light kiss on the lips.

A tall, broad woman wearing a maxi length dark coat walked past. She had long, black hair and looked pretty odd to me, reminding me of someone who dressed up as a woman — someone like Danny La Rue.

Jude noticed her too and we both laughed and shook our heads at some of the sights you see now on the streets in

London. I told him then about the light-bulb moment that I'd had, about Dennis Simpson stalking me for my money.

'Yeah, that could well be the case. Obviously he feels he should benefit from his mum and dad as well. But the thing is, Esther, his mum and dad didn't know whether he was dead or alive and, legally, the house was left to you, so it's your money. He hasn't a leg to stand on if he tries his luck at getting some of it.'

I nodded as he went on to say, 'He lives in their house now anyway. He must have money.'

'Maybe he just rents it!'

'Maybe so.'

'Anyway,' I said, 'to get him off my back I'd let him have it all.'

'Don't be too hasty, Esther, you may have need of that money someday.' He squeezed my hand. 'And anyway, he won't be needing any soon — not when we find him and he gets banged up for kidnap.' He raised his eyebrows.

'OK, I'll wait and see what happens.'

'Anyway,' he tipped his head back to

drain his mug, 'as much as I'd like to stay here all day talking with you, I've some follow-up work to do on that new case.'

'Yeah, and I was thinking of visiting Martha.'

* * *

The rain was still coming down in long, sharp needles, hitting the ground with force, splashing against my legs and my boots, as we kissed goodbye under The Milk Maid's awning. His lips felt warm and moist against mine, and his stubble scratchy on my skin. A couple of young men made comments as they sauntered by, to which Jude fixed them with his blindingly blue stare until they shut their mouths and scurried away.

Abandoning my thoughts of visiting Martha at London Girl — I'd get soaked through on the way — I decided to go up to my flat to get warm. I'd call Martha later, from the phone box in the hallway.

Once inside, I shrugged off my coat and went straight into the kitchen to put the kettle on to boil. The gas spurted into life, a little blue flame that widened across the bottom of the kettle as I placed it on the hob.

I busied myself with getting a mug, coffee, sugar and milk but, as the kettle was getting ready to boil, the room filling with steam, I heard something behind me. I spun around, suddenly spooked, the hairs on the back of my neck prickling.

My heart gave an almighty heave as a voice said, 'Hello Esther baby.' Whoever it was gave a little giggle. 'Bet you never expected to see me here, did you?'

'Who the hell are you?' I said, as I came face to face with the woman I'd seen walk past the window of The Milk Maid earlier — the big woman with long black hair, the woman Jude and I had laughed at. I shrank back against the worktop as the kettle came to the boil, shrieking like someone in pain. Quickly I turned off the gas. I was confused and trembling — the voice, deep as a man's, not matching what I could see.

'Recognise me now?'

The 'woman' suddenly ripped off her long black hair to reveal that 'she' was bald as a newborn baby, her head a perfect egg shape. 'Oh Esther, you must recognise me now?'

His eyes were still piggy and blue, not the vibrant blue of Jude's, but cloudy and red rimmed, ominous somehow, just as I'd thought before. He laughed as he waved the wig in the air and then, pulling at the black dress, removed that too and dumped it all on the floor. He stood there then in jeans and a T-shirt, a long-sleeved one hiding the snake tattoo that I knew would still be slithering around and around his arm beneath the thin material.

'You! But . . .' I swallowed, my throat feeling small and scratchy. 'How did you get in?'

'Locks are easy to pick. Especially flimsy ones like yours.'

'But the door was deadlocked!'

'Oh yeah? Is that your only door, Esther baby?'

The fire door. Reached from outside by a clanking metal staircase. He grinned.

'Ah yeah, I can almost see your brain whirring. The fire door, yeah, the fire door . . . easy-peasy to get in. You need to tell your landlord to tighten up his security.'

Shrinking back against the worktop, I said, 'What do you want?'

He took a step towards me and I shrank back even further.

'Coffee? Oh, you're just making some, I see. Any for me?'

Turning around, my heart pumping, I took another mug from the cupboard and put a spoonful of coffee in it. My hands were shaking despite my attempts to appear calm and some spilled on the worktop.

'Sugar?' I asked.

'Oh, two for me please, Esther baby,' he said in a silly high-pitched voice. 'Hey, I bet you were worried for your little friend, Julie, weren't you, huh?'

I carried on calmly making the drinks.

'No, I knew we'd get her back. The police are on to you, make no mistake. Even though you tried to frame Marty Valesko, saying that Julie went home with him.'

He gave a deep, throaty chuckle.

'Who cares about Marty Valesko, eh? I bet he'd have liked to go home with her. Stop grasping at straws, Esther baby, the police will never get me. They didn't even know it was me today, did they? I saw them, but they didn't see me. Oh no.'

Knowing that this was true but losing patience and suddenly filled with bravado, I turned to face him.

'What do you want, Dennis? If it's money, I can get you some...'

'Money?' he repeated. 'Oh yeah, don't we all want money! But I want my life back, Esther baby. The life I should have had if those sorry excuses for parents hadn't stolen me away from it.'

I shook my head.

'How do you expect me to do that,

Dennis? I wasn't even born when you were stolen from your pram.'

'I didn't even know until she was on her death bed. She told me everything then. He told me nothing . . . he was a waste of space.' He kept rambling on. 'You had all the best years, the best years with my mum and dad. They were *my* mum and dad, not yours!'

He sounded like a petulant child. I almost expected him to burst into tears.

'They were my mum and dad too, Dennis,' I said as calmly as I could. 'I knew nothing about you, they didn't tell me what had happened, that their child, my brother, was stolen away from them —'

He began to laugh, an awful manic laugh, a laugh that sent shivers down my spine.

'Oh, so you think I'm your brother, do you?' he said, gasping and wiping his eyes with his fingers.

'Well . . . it's the only thing I can come up with.'

My heart thumped and I could feel

sweat prickling everywhere, under my arms, at the back of my neck. Even my palms felt wet and slimy.

'We look nothing alike,' he said. 'I mean, look at you, Grace Kelly to a tee and me . . . ha. . . . Well, who do I resemble? Herman Munster?'

'Not all brothers and sisters look alike,' I said.

'Are you stupid?' he said, coming a step closer to me, making me shrink back even more, trying to make myself as small as possible. 'What if they weren't your mum and dad? Yeah, what about that, then? What if you were adopted?'

'But I'm not,' I said tearfully. 'They were my mum and dad just as much as they were yours.'

'If you were adopted though, Esther baby,' he said slyly, his piggy eyes glinting, 'their house wasn't yours to sell, it's mine. I'm the true born child.'

'Yeah, that's OK,' I told him. 'I still have all the money. You can have it, I promise.'

'I want my life back!' he screamed as he lunged towards me. 'It's all your fault they're dead…'

Unknowingly, he'd touched a nerve, a very raw nerve and tears threatened.

Sick to the back teeth of this menacing conversation, and wanting out as soon as I could, I remembered the story Jude had told me about pepper. Quick as a flash I reached for the pepper pot which was on the worktop with the salt and, ripping out the plug at the bottom, flung the contents into his face.

Immediately he backed away, screaming, and put his hands over his eyes giving me the opportunity to make a run for it.

I dashed from the kitchen and flinging open the door, raced down the stairs and outside onto the pavement where the rain was still belting down in sheets and streaming along the gutters like hundreds of tiny silver fish. I ran to the police car, and banged on the window, where the two police men were lounging back in their seats, eating burgers and listening to some catchy music on the radio.

'For God's sake,' I shouted at them. 'Dennis Simpson's up in my flat.' I pointed to the open doorway as they both threw down their burgers and leapt from the car, rushing straight into the building.

A couple of minutes later they came thundering down the stairs, holding Dennis Simpson handcuffed between them, his eyes red and swollen. He tried to break away from the officers, lurching menacingly towards me, but I stepped back out of his grasp.

One of the officers pushed him head first into the back of the car while the other apologised profusely for letting him get past them.

'We only saw a woman with long black hair,' he said, looking puzzled.

'Yeah,' I said, shivering under The Milk Maid's awning. I was soaked through, my clothes stuck to me and my hair hung in rat's tails down my shoulders and my back. 'That was him. Cunningly disguised.'

'Wow,' he said, shaking his head. 'Well, he sure had us fooled.'

Dripping wet now, water sliding off their hats, both officers gave a two-finger salute at their temple, got quickly into the car and drove away.

I could just about see the outline of Dennis Simpson in the back. He didn't turn around, probably wouldn't be able to see me anyway, with those red-rimmed eyes. Hysterical laughter started to bubble up inside me.

A car pulled up with a screech at the kerb and someone got out, closing the door with a thunk behind them. It was raining so hard now, I could barely see who it was, just a man holding his hat on his head with one hand and running towards me.

'Esther?'

'Jude?'

He took me into his arms, pressing my wet body tight against him.

'I had a feeling something wasn't right,' he said, 'that I should check on you. Boy, I'm glad I did. He got into your flat somehow, didn't he?'

I nodded, worn out now with fatigue and shock but relieved that Jude was here with me. I was nervous of going into my flat alone.

'Just to let you know,' I said, 'the pepper worked!'

He smiled, a great broad smile.

'I knew one of my stories would come in useful some day.'

'Thank God, the police have got him now.'

'Hey, come on.' He put his arm around my shoulders. 'You're soaked through. I'll see you inside.'

Stumbling a bit on the stairs, we disappeared inside out of the driving rain.

* * *

Jude sat in on the police interview with Dennis Simpson. We'd arranged to meet in Leopold's afterwards, where he filled me in on all the details.

It was early evening and Leopold's was buzzing. People were enjoying tasty-looking chicken and chips in a basket and beer and wine. The juke box was playing and I hummed along, tapping my foot in time to the music. The Supremes were one of my favourites. *Stop in the name of love, before you break my heart.*

The smell of fried food, alcohol and perfume hung in the air. Jude came back from the bar carrying a pint with a creamy head and a Babycham. I recognised the long-stemmed glass with the cute Bambi on the front straight away.

'Hey,' I said, 'I blamed Marty Valesko last time for the effects of this drink. Hope I'm not blaming you this time.'

He grinned and said, 'One or two won't harm you . . . and anyway you deserve it, with all you've been through.'

Baby, baby, I'm aware of where you go, each time you leave my door, I watch you walk down the street, knowing your other love you'll meet . . .

I smiled at him and took a sip, feeling the heady bubbles pop in my mouth and even up my nose.

'Hmm,' I said, licking my lips. 'Sweet and lovely.'

'Yeah — just like you,' he said looking at me fondly with his hot blue eyes. 'I like your little dress too.'

My shift dress was green and short, teamed with white tights and black knee-length boots.

'And you are too,' I said shyly.

But this time before you run to her, leaving me alone and hurt (think it over) . . .

'Hey, boys aren't sweet and lovely, are they?'

'Not all of them, but you are. Anyway, come on.' I nudged him with my elbow and he moved up closer on the seat, his thigh touching mine. 'Fill me in on what happened with Dennis Simpson.'

After I've been to you? (think it over), after I've been sweet to you . . .

He took a sip of his pint and said, 'He sure is a weird one. When he was asked, 'Why did you kidnap Julie Foster?' he answered, 'Because I could. Because she was there.' Jude shook his head, a wry twist to his lips. 'But he did admit later that it was his way of getting to you. He knew that you worked with her and that it would upset and scare you. After all, he had to get your attention somehow, didn't he?'

'He actually admitted that?'

Jude nodded and sipped at this drink.

'He also said that he couldn't believe it when he saw you in Milly's. Apparently he'd never seen you in a place like that before and knew then that his job of getting revenge on you would be a lot easier.'

'Revenge?'

Stop in the name of love, before you break my heart . . .

'Yeah, a strange word to use . . . as though you were responsible for taking away his life with his mum and dad, and not his abductors. It's like . . .' He thought for a moment or two. 'Like being abducted turned his mind somehow.' He shrugged. 'Or maybe he would have grown up to be the way he is anyway. Who knows?'

'Maybe he's looking for someone to

blame?'

I've known of your, your secluded nights, I've even see her, maybe once or twice . . .

Jude shrugged and said, 'Maybe . . .'

There was a short silence where we gazed at each other and then I said, 'Did he say anything about me being adopted?'

Jude frowned. 'No! Why?'

'That's what he said to me.' I conjured him up again, standing in my kitchen, his face and head like a great featureless, sweaty moon. *What if they weren't your mum and dad*? *What if you were adopted, Esther*?

'He also said that it was my fault they were dead and that he was the true born child!'

I could barely swallow, my throat felt so tight, and tears, salty and hot threatened to fall.

But is her sweet expression worth more than my love and affection?

Jude winced and, squeezing my hand tightly, said, 'He hit a nerve there, didn't he? I'm glad you caught him right in the eyes with the pepper! You should have chucked the pot at him as well. The truth of the matter, though, Esther, is that he knows nothing of the details about your mum and dad's deaths, nothing! What's with the adoption thing though and this true born child idea? Maybe he's delusional!'

I shook my head. 'I don't know. I just hope it's not something else they failed to tell me. After all, Dennis is right in what he said . . . he and I don't look alike enough for a brother and sister, and although Mum and Dad never said anything, I was always aware I didn't look like them at all.'

'Aah,' said Jude dismissively, waving a hand. 'It's all in the family genes, you probably look a lot like . . . I don't know, your great great grandma or Great-aunt Doris. Great beauties in their day, having been gifted with thick ash-blonde hair and Bette Davis eyes. Oh, and a perfect hourglass figure too . . .' He pushed up closer and put an arm around my shoulders.

'Esther,' he whispered in my ear making me shiver. 'Remember what I asked you a while ago and I said I was going to ask you again?'

His hot breath warmed my neck and I felt as if I could melt right into him, soft and creamy, like an ice cream on a hot summer day.

'Yes?' I said, looking straight into his eyes, blue and brown locked.

'Well, Esther . . . I know it's not the ideal place to ask you, but will you—'

'Hey, if it isn't the beautiful Esther Chambers and her sidekick, Jude Dunbar! Please, it would give me great pleasure to buy you both a drink.'

Shocked by this great bellowing voice interrupting what was a very private moment, we reluctantly tore our gaze away from one another, to look straight into the mischievous dancing eyes of Marty Valesko.

9

It's Sunday, I thought lazily, as I turned over and burrowed deeper like a little mole into the cosy warmth of the blankets. *I don't have to get up yet. There's no rush . . . I've all the time in the world.*

I sighed contentedly. The bedroom was gloomy with just a faint lemon light trying to edge its way around the curtains. The wardrobe stood like a vast black shadow against the wall, suddenly giving me the spooks and bringing back the shock I'd felt on the night when Dennis Simpson had decided to pay me a visit.

His pasty round moonface surrounded by the deep black of the long wig was like something in a scary film, and the creepy snake tattoo revealed on the arm of a man wearing a woman's dress was now to me the ultimate stuff of nightmares.

Hey, move over Truman Capote, I

bet I could write a true horror story almost as good as yours with just one character — Dennis Simpson.

Thoughts of last night in Leopold's in the company of Jude and Marty Valesko ran through my mind and, moving my head slightly on the pillow, was relieved that I was able to lift it. The last time I'd been with Marty Valesko, my head had felt like a ten-ton weight the day after and I'd blamed him for buying me too many sweet, bubbly Babycham drinks. Of course it wasn't my fault for drinking them, oh no, he plied me with them, tortured me into drinking them!

I recalled his shock when we told him that it was none other than the barman at Milly's, Dennis Simpson, who had kidnapped Julie and that also, everything was pointing to the probability that he and I had had the same parents. Marty had been working away truck driving for the past week so knew nothing of this, having seen no local papers and, obviously, hadn't been frequenting Milly's at all to catch up on any newsworthy gossip.

'Wow,' he exclaimed, his dark eyes sparkling. 'You mean the snatched baby is your brother? Wow! But you don't look anything alike!'

A group of people came to sit at the table next to ours, talking and laughing as they put their drinks on the table. The jukebox thumped and Mick Jagger's sexily strident voice could clearly be heard over the hum of voices.

'Yeah, we've already thought about that,' Jude said, as he took a sip of his creamy headed pint.

'Jude thinks I might be a throwback and maybe look like my Great-aunt Doris,' I put in.

'Well, I don't know about Great-aunt Doris,' said Marty Valesko, 'but you've got the look of Grace Kelly and eyes like Bette Davis . . . what a combination.'

'Hey, hey, not so fast there, man. This girl is mine.' Grinning, Jude put a protective arm tightly around my shoulders and pulled me close.

'That's exactly what Dennis Simpson

said,' I told them. 'He said that I looked like Grace Kelly and who did he look like but Herman Munster!'

Marty Valesko laughed long and loud, and then drained the rest of his pint in one gulp.

'Yeah, you know, thinking about it, he's not wrong! Herman Munster, huh? The beauty and the beast!' And then turning to Jude, and waving a dismissive hand, he said, 'I wouldn't steal your girl, I got one of my own.' When we leaned towards him with interest, he added, 'One in every port, I mean...'

Coming back to the present, I got out of bed and, shrugging on my dressing gown, padded over to the window and peered through the curtains.

My heart lifted at the sight of the sun shining in a clear sky with just a few white fluffy clouds floating about in the blue. A blue as bright and sparkling as Jude's eyes. The rain had stopped for now and, oh my, what a lovely sight.

Slipping on my fluffy mules I clip-clopped to the kitchen where I lit the gas and, filling up the kettle, set it on the stove to boil, peering over my shoulder, my heart thumping, to check that Dennis Simpson, wearing a long black dress and a wig, wasn't standing behind me.

The kettle screeched to the boil and, pouring water into a mug, I thought that maybe it was time to think about moving. I certainly didn't feel the same about living in this place as I did before Dennis Simpson broke in. I needed new locks, that was for sure; 'flimsy' ones as he'd said mine were, were an open invitation to an intruder. I may as well have asked him to come in and have coffee with me.

I could afford to move. I had money stashed away, although yeah, I'd told Dennis Simpson he could have it all . . . and he still could. But I had my wage from Jude, which was more than I'd been paid at Attitude, so, yeah, I'd start looking around at other places. I'd start tomorrow, I decided. Monday.

Moving into the sitting room, I stood at the window, absent-mindedly sipping my coffee, watching people walking along the street, wondering where they were going, what they were going to do today. Maybe Sunday lunch and a drink or two in a pub, the weather was good enough for a walk in the park.

A sudden thought hit me. *What if Marty Valesko hadn't turned up last night, would I be an engaged woman by now? Was Jude going to propose? I mean, seriously propose? What would I have said anyway . . . would I have said yes?*

I took another sip of coffee and thought, *Yeah, do you know what? I think I would. I couldn't imagine my life without him now.*

How had that happened? I had a good feeling with Jude. He appreciated me not only for my looks but my brain too, which was a rare thing in a man. And of course he had many other charms, far too numerous to count.

The usual white van pulled up at the kerb and the muscular guy with the grin got out and started unloading pallets of fresh bread, massive tins of coffee, bags of sugar, bags of tea and hundreds of cartons of milk. There was a faint thump, thump as someone put a record on the jukebox. I swayed from side to side to the beat.

A loud voice broke into my thoughts, winding its way up the stairs.

'Hey, Esther, the phone for you. This early on a Sunday morning? Is this guy joking, you know?'

Smiling to myself, I put my coffee mug down and, tying my dressing gown tighter around my waist, ran down the stairs. Tony held the receiver out to me, a wide grin splitting his face in two.

'And she comes down half naked!' He put out a palm to shield his face.

'Hey,' I chided him, playfully poking him in the ribs. I took the receiver from him as I held my dressing gown tightly at the neck with one hand.

'Esther baby, if a guy rings so early in the morning, that means he loves you, you know? Soon you'll be married with six kids driving you crazy, all screaming in your face at once.'

I shook my head at him, as he walked,

laughing, into the kitchens, the guy from the van brushing past me, dumping all the stuff on the worktops and the floor.

'Hello?'

'Esther?'

'Hi. You're early.'

'Yeah, well, what do they say? The early bird catches the worm!'

'I ain't no worm,' I said indignantly.

His soft laughter tickled my ears sending shivers running down my spine.

'Come out with me today?'

'What have you got in mind?'

'A run out in the car . . . find a little pub somewhere. The sun is shining, not a cloud in the sky, it's sweet enough to sit outside.' He started to sing, '*Oh what a beautiful morning, oh what a beautiful day . . .*'

'OK, OK,' I said. 'What time? I'm not even dressed yet.'

'Oh Esther, not dressed? Don't you be filling my mind with those sort of thoughts, not so early on a Sunday morning. *I've got a beautiful feeling, everything's going my way . . .*'

'Jude!'

'An hour? Can you be ready in an hour?'

'Yes!'

I ran back up the stairs, my fluffy mules clip clopping on every step, the sound of Tony's voice shouting backwards and forwards with the muscular guy and the incessant thump of the jukebox following me all the way. Rushing into the bathroom, I turned on the taps for a bath, hurrying to get ready for Jude.

* * *

We sped along the country lanes in Jude's car, eating up the miles like somebody nibbling on a length of liquorice, leaving London and all its built up areas of houses and shops well behind us.

I glanced at Jude from the corner of my eye, at the stubble on his cheeks and chin, at his bright blue eyes steady on the road. He reached out a hand and squeezed my thigh, making me feel soft and fluid as if my whole body was sinking into the car seat like melted chocolate.

Spring had arrived at last and the daffodils bloomed like bright spots of gold along grass verges, cows and sheep chewed contentedly on grass, and yellow fields of rapeseed flew by in a blur.

Like a dream come true, the sun shone in an arched sky of blue and twittering birds flew overhead in amongst the fluffy clouds. All my worries of the previous weeks fled away as if they'd never happened; the trauma of Julie going missing and the constant bullying from Pam, and subsequently being fired from my job.

But the terror of being alone in my flat when Dennis Simpson broke in still made me shiver, and there was the nagging worry that every word he said could be true, as with a sinking heart I realised that my mum and dad might not really have been mine, and that somewhere out there my real parents could be looking for me, trying to find me, just as desperately as we had tried to find Julie.

Oh, how fanciful I was being. Why on

earth would I believe the vindictive words of someone like Dennis Simpson? After all, what was that saying about people who lied? *He who lies does not do so for gain, but just to amuse himself.* Yes, he was probably laughing right now at the fear of God he'd instilled in me.

'Esther?'

I came back to earth, sucked out of my thoughts as if I'd been deep inside a dream, at the sound of Jude's voice.

'Wow, where were you, Esther baby?'

We were stopped in a layby overlooking fields of sheep, horses and cows, all grazing peacefully.

'Oh! sorry, I was miles away, in a dream. Thinking about Dennis Simpson.'

'Ah,' said Jude, waving dismissively. 'Don't think about him today. Today is for enjoyment only. Come with me.'

Getting out of the car, he went to the boot, emerging with a picnic basket and a blanket.

'Jude! Why didn't you tell me we were picnicking?'

‘It was a last minute thought,’ he said easily. ‘Only sandwiches, cake,’ and added with a glint in his eye, ‘and Babycham . . .’

‘Babycham?’

‘Oh yes. Come with me, Esther baby, and you won’t go far wrong.’

We sat in the dappled shade of a tree, the sun glinting through the leaves so they shone bright green, sending out lozenges of light onto the blanket and onto our skin. The sun beat down warm and heavy as a bowl of yellow custard, and the smell of cut grass and hay hung in the air. Somewhere a dog barked and we heard the faraway clucking of chickens and the harsh crowing of a rooster. We ate the sandwiches and cake and once again I found myself inhaling the bubbles of the Babycham as they popped in my mouth and up my nose.

Jude took off his jacket and folding it, laid it on the grass like a pillow. Sated, we lay back on the blanket, our fingers entwined, as the long drowsy day unfolded.

Jude turned on his side towards me and whispered closely in my ear, his breath tickling my neck and making me squirm.

'I don't think Marty Valesko will interrupt us this time, Esther . . . do you?'

Before I could reply, he stood up and, fumbling in his pocket, dipped down onto one knee. In shock, I sat up and stared at him, my hands to my neck and my heart thumping like a train gathering speed on its way out of a station. He knelt, one hand on his heart, the other holding a tiny box.

'Esther, my darling Esther. It has to be said that over the past few months I have found a very high regard for you…'

Stifling laughter, I said, 'Oh, Jude!'

'And would ask you here on bended knee for you to take me as your husband…'

'Oh, Jude . . .' Tears burned right at the very back of my eyes.

'Will you answer yay or nay?' he enquired imperiously.

Like the bubbles in the Babycham,

laughter rose up in me, threatening to burst at any moment.

'I say yay!'

'You will? You'll marry me? Wow . . . holy cow!'

Shyly I nodded as he opened the little box and, carefully removing the ring, slowly slid it on to my finger.

'And now I'm truly happy,' he said as his warm lips met mine and his kiss, slow and languid as the hot day, made my heart beat faster.

Snaking my arm around his neck, I pulled him closer, lightly cupping the back of his head with my palm. His lips tasted sweet and bubbly as the Babycham.

* * *

It was late when we arrived back at The Milk Maid, street lights shining in an orange glow onto the pavements and the sky arching above us sprinkled with millions of tiny stars. With sinking hearts we pulled up at the kerb behind a police car, blue lights flashing.

'Oh no,' I said. 'What could have happened?' Thoughts that something might have happened to Tony, Marie, or a customer in The Milk Maid flashed through my mind.

'I'll go find out,' said Jude as he got out of the car and walked over to the two policemen. The same two I noticed that had been there on the night that Dennis Simpson had broken into my flat.

I watched the three of them talking. There was much shaking of heads and gestures with their hands. Jude looked angry as he glanced around where I still sat in the car, unable to move, rooted to the spot.

I wound the window down, the odour of fried food and coffee immediately flooding into the car from the Milk Maid's open door, as Jude walked back towards me.

'Esther — I think you had better come and stay at my place tonight.'

I looked at him questioningly until, taking a deep breath, he said, 'Dennis Simpson has got out of prison. It's not safe for you here.'

'What? Escaped? Oh my God . . . no!'

'Yeah . . . how did they allow that to happen, eh?'

The steady thump thump from the jukebox echoed out onto the street

We've already said goodbye, since you've got to go, oh you'd better go now, go now, go now . . .

'You'd better go in and get an overnight bag though, OK?'

I felt shaken and worried as I nodded and got out of the car. The two policemen murmured platitudes to me about how sorry they were and that for now, maybe I'd be better staying elsewhere. 'Dennis Simpson knows where you live, ma'am . . .'

I nodded to them as I walked past and clattered up the stairs to my flat to pack a bag.

I was conscious of the engagement ring on my finger and the lovely day that we'd shared and now to come home to this. They were right though, I needed to get away from here; the thought of being in close proximity to Dennis Simpson filled me with dread. And the irony of the song playing, as if the Moody Blues knew of my plight. *We've already said so long, I don't want to see you go*, oh, *you'd better go now . . .*

Putting a few things into an overnight bag, I switched off all the lights and, locking the door firmly behind me, ran down the stairs and outside into the cool, dark night.

10

Do you think he might be holed up in Norfolk Terrace?' I asked Jude the following morning as we sat in the sitting room of his flat looking through the paper at adverts for flats to rent.

I took a sip of strong, hot coffee. Jude's place was cool, a one-bedroom flat with a large, bright and airy sitting room, black and white arty pictures displayed on white-painted walls. He had a really nice comfortable settee, all squashy brown leather, with two matching chairs. He also had a colour television, which was virtually unheard of — 'imported from America,' Jude told me — a fancy record player with a glass lid and his very own private telephone. Wow, living the high life, as Martha would have said.

He shrugged and said, 'Well, if he's intelligent enough, you'd think he'd know better than to go there. But then again he's busted out of prison, which is a very stupid thing to do. I still can't believe it!' He made a few red circles with a pen on the newspaper. 'Somebody inside must have helped him. There were no broken locks and no one saw anything. It's a mystery.'

'He's not human,' I said with distaste. 'He slithers in and out of places just like the snake tattoo on his arm . . . ugh.'

Jude laughed throwing his head back revealing his long tanned neck and the mat of chest hair on display above the open buttons of his shirt. To distract myself, I pointed to the red pen circles on the paper.

'What have you seen?'

'Hmm, a couple of places that might suit you. Do you want to go and take a look at them?'

I nodded as he looked at me eyebrows raised.

'I need a furnished place…'

'Yeah, that's fine, most places for rent are furnished.' Moving closer he drew me into his arms, his mouth finding my neck. 'Not that I wouldn't rather you stayed here.' And then, 'Wow, that's a really fancy ring you're wearing . . .'

Splaying my hand out in front of me, I wiggled my fingers around.

'Yeah, fancy . . . and very special.' We shared a look before I said, 'If I stayed here, I think you'd soon get fed up with sleeping on the settee every night.'

He shook his head as I whispered in his ear, 'I think we should go take a look at Norfolk Terrace on our way out, don't you?'

* * *

The police were sitting in their car outside number ten, Norfolk Terrace when we pulled up at the kerb. I gazed up at the house, its windows blank and lifeless as Dennis Simpson's eyes. One of the officers wandered over and peered in through the open window. It was a sunny day again but with a chill in the air, the blue sky smeared with smoky tendrils of clouds. Even here, surrounded by houses, streets and roads, birds sang their joyful spring chorus reminding me of our special day yesterday in the countryside.

'Hey, there.' The officer nodded at us, and explained that they were keeping the house under surveillance for any sightings of Derek Simpson and would let us know if there were any comings or goings or any other unexplained movements.

Jude nodded saying, 'Yeah, cool, you know how to get me.' He brandished his walkie talkie as if it was a toy.

'Don't forget to look out for men dressed as women,' I teased the officer.

He gave an embarrassed grin and ducked his head.

'I don't think I'll ever do that again, ma'am.'

'I hope not,' I said, 'I may joke, officer, but I'm scared. Dennis Simpson is on the loose.'

'I know, ma'am, don't worry, we'll take care of him. And you.'

Full of misgivings I whispered to Jude as the officer walked back to his car, 'Maybe we should have taken a look inside ourselves. After all, they didn't look after me before, did they?'

He shrugged, looking in the mirror with narrowed eyes before pulling out into the steady stream of traffic.

'Yeah, well, Laurel and Hardy back there haven't seen him going in or out, so we'd better let them get on with it for the time being. No doubt they've been inside to check anyway.'

'Maybe we should have told them that the key's under the mat?'

He grinned and said, 'What's the first place I've circled in red?' nodding towards the newspaper that I'd laid across my lap.

'Wow, it's Richmond Villas! That's where Martha lives. Why didn't you say?'

'I don't know who Martha is, let alone where she lives, Esther baby.'

* * *

As we pulled up outside, I gazed at Richmond Villas, a tall pale brick 1930s building, set with tall windows and balconies.

'Wow,' I said. 'No wonder Martha has her own telephone, living in a place like this. Maybe out of my price range, Jude...'

Jude gazed at the building, his eyes narrowed, assessing.

'Hmm, no harm in looking. Come on.'

Martha came out of the revolving door just as we were about to enter. To my eyes she looked as reassuring as ever, wearing her good black coat, even though it was a warm day, and carrying her heavy bag. She started when she saw me and gave a smile that split her face in two.

'Hey, Esther baby. What you doing here?'

'Martha!' I flung my arms around her, pulling her close, feeling the roughness of her coat against my cheek. For some reason, I felt close to tears. 'Wow, it's so good to see you too . . . I, I mean we,' I pointed to Jude, 'have come to look at a flat to rent. Not together, um . . . just me.' Flustered, I said, 'Jude — this is Martha Engleson. We worked together at Attitude. Martha, this is Jude Dunbar.'

'Oh yeah, the Paul Newman lookalike. Pleased to meet you.' She held out her hand and shook Jude's strong and hard.

'Pleased to meet you, Martha.' He shook his head, puzzled. 'Paul Newman?'

'Yeah, you got the twinkle,' she said, pointing to her eyes.

Discreetly I showed Martha my ring.

'Oh, Esther baby, didn't I tell you there'd be wedding bells?' And then turning to Jude, 'You got the best here, you know. You take care of her, eh?'

Jude put a protective arm around my shoulders,

'Yeah, I will. And you'll be the first on our invitation list when those bells do ring, Martha.'

'I'd be honoured,' she said. I could tell how pleased she was by the emphatic nod of her head before she turned to me. 'Why you wanting to move, Esther baby? I thought you liked Tony at the Milk Maid.'

'Oh, I do . . .' I filled her in on everything that had happened with Dennis Simpson. 'I just don't feel safe there any more, Martha.'

'Yeah, you're doing the right thing. If he gets a chance, he'll take you like he took Julie.' She glanced at her watch, 'Hey, I'd like to stay all day but I gotta go to work or I'll be late. Ring me.'

She gave the usual phone gesture, a hand to the ear, thumb and little finger outspread.

I watched her waddle away, so small and dumpy yet with a heart twice the size of almost anyone I'd ever known.

Jude caught hold of my hand as we entered the building and, going to the reception desk, we explained why we were there. After a phone call, the landlord appeared. A tall, distinguished man with grey hair, he let us into the flat and then discreetly disappeared so we had the place to ourselves.

It was big — a lot bigger than my place over The Milk Maid.

'Two of my place could fit in here,' I said as I looked around in awe.

The flat was on the third floor, and in the sitting room, a large bay window looked out onto the busy street below and all the people scurrying along like ants. Just like The Milk Maid, it was near enough to the centre of town to walk there in maybe ten minutes.

There was a balcony at the back through the bedroom which overlooked the beautifully kept communal gardens, which today were glowing green and yellow and red in the blinding sunshine.

'No more thump-thump from the jukebox,' I said as I opened the doors and stepped out onto the balcony, taking deep breaths of the fresh spring air. The sun felt warm and soft on my skin.

'Or the smell of everyone's fried breakfasts drifting up the stairs,' said Jude, coming to stand beside me, snaking his arm around my waist. He'd lit a cigarette and the acrid smell of the smoke circled around us.

'Oh . . . Tony will be sad though, when I tell him I'm going.'

'Tony will be fine. He'll just get another tenant.'

'No . . . he likes me.'

'Ah,' said Jude, grinning and waving his hand dismissively. 'A tenant's a tenant.'

'Cynic!' I said, nudging him hard in the ribs.

'Softy!' He nudged me back.

'But do you know what will be best of all?' I asked, pointing at the phone on the bedside cabinet. 'I won't have to freeze half to death while making a phone call. As Martha said, I'm living the high life.'

Jude pulled me closer.

'I can call you day or night . . . night or day . . . what's that song? *Night and day, you are the one, only you beneath the moon, under the sun . . .*'

I grinned and said lightly, 'You interfere with my beauty sleep and I'll report you for harassment.'

'You don't need beauty sleep,' Jude crooned lightly, nibbling at my neck and my ear before saying, 'Do you wanna look anywhere else? There were a few red circles on that paper.'

'No,' I said. 'This is the place for me. Especially with Martha being here too, it makes me feel safe — and with the high salary you pay me, I can afford it.'

He laughed long and loud, releasing me then grabbing my hand.

'Come on then, let's go and sort out all the details with the landlord. And then maybe you can come with me today?'

I looked at him questioningly, eyebrows raised.

'I'm going to visit Suzanne again. She rang me last night and said she's found some papers that belonged to her mother that might help with tracking down her adopted sister. If you really want to earn that high salary and move in to this place, come with me and take notes.'

'Huh, you strike a hard bargain Jude

Dunbar,' I said as I kissed his stubbly chin.

'Hey, Esther baby . . . you stick with me and you're on the right track.'

* * *

I awoke suddenly. It was dark and, just for a split second, I had no idea where I was. Then everything came crashing into my mind and I remembered that I was in bed in my flat above The Milk Maid.

There was silence, a deep, dark silence and my heart hammered in my breast. I felt suffocated in the thick blackness as if I couldn't breathe. I closed my eyes and took several deep breaths willing myself to go back to sleep but Derek Simpson's moronic face flashed into my thoughts making it an impossible task.

Sitting up, I reached out a shaky hand and switched on the bedside lamp. A soft pink glow flooded the room.

Shrugging on my dressing gown and pushing my feet into slippers, I padded into the kitchen and put the kettle on the stove to boil. There was no point in trying to go back to sleep, I had too much on my mind. Shivering, I took a mug from the cupboard, got coffee and milk, all the time glancing over my shoulder, fearful of someone standing there, someone evil and menacing clad in a long black dress and a wig. Yeah, maybe it would be better when I was out of this place.

And yet, after telling Tony the somewhat sad news, he had said, arms out wide, 'Hey Esther baby, good news for you . . . bad news for me.'

'You know why I'm going, don't you?' I'd asked him quietly.

'Yeah, the bad guy. He shouldn't have got in. My security is the tightest it's ever been now.'

'Tony, it says twenty-eight days' notice in the contract, but can I give fourteen? It's too dangerous and worrying for me to stay any longer than that.'

He'd flung his arms around me, and then pulled back, his hands cupping my shoulders.

'You're a good tenant . . . the best I've ever had. Fourteen days is cool. All I want is your safety.'

'Thank you, Tony — you've always been good to me.'

He threw up his hands. 'Oh Esther baby, I don't want you to go. I'm going to lose the customers that only come here to see your pretty face.'

'Flatterer,' I had said to him, laughing.

Going into the sitting room now, I sat on the settee, hunched forward, sipping from my mug, the hot coffee reviving me a little, turning my thoughts away from Tony and to the visit yesterday with Jude to see his new client, Suzanne.

On our way, we'd driven along Carnaby Street where we got stuck in a build-up of traffic and the crowds of people spreading out all over the road and ogling the live models in the window of London Girl. Jude had to press down hard on the car horn to get them to move out the way.

'Wow, look at all this,' I said. 'All because of live models. Jo, one of Attitude's models, was taken away by the police for doing this very thing.'

'What harm are they doing? It's no different from the modelling you did inside, is it?'

'I agree in most ways, but have you seen what they're wearing? They're almost naked!'

'What's wrong with that?' said Jude, a grin hovering around his lips.

'Hmm, you would say that!'

* * *

'Are we here?' I asked peering from the window as we pulled up outside a narrow terraced house, sandwiched between houses on either side like a filling between two slices of bread. The street was long and narrow with the exact same houses on the other side, as if they were reflected in a mirror.

There was an unmade rutted road in between and mature trees with thick trunks grew on the grass verges, remnants from the dense forest that had been here many years before.

The front door, which faced straight onto the pavement, was a shiny black and the door knocker gleamed. It brought back images of Mum bustling around with her polish and her yellow duster flicking at imaginary specks of dust.

'We sure are. Fifty-six, Lord Street.'

Jude knocked on the door and Suzanne, on opening up, welcomed us with a smile. Yet I noticed a subtle, frightened search with her eyes up and down the street, as she ushered us in and quickly closed the door.

'Jude Dunbar . . . again,' said Jude with a grin, flashing his ID towards her. 'This time with my assistant, Esther Chambers. Is everything OK?'

'Pleased to meet you,' she said, shaking my hand. 'Yeah, but there's been someone hanging about outside for the past couple of days and, well . . .' Momentarily sidetracked, she said to me, 'You've obviously been told before that you look a lot like Grace Kelly?'

I nodded and said, 'Yeah,' and she giggled as she led us from a tiny hallway with the stairs leading up in front of us into a small sitting room. A real fire was burning, the flames roaring like a lion up the chimney for, even though it was warm outside, it was shady and cool in here.

The house smelled fresh and clean with a faint undertone of baking, as if she'd been making something sweet like biscuits or puddings. There was the smell of soot, too, from the fire and some very nice coffee, as if she had a percolator in the kitchen. Very upmarket — putting me to shame with my boiled water and instant.

She was very pretty, her ash-blonde hair cut into a chin-length bob, with dark make-up around the eyes and a sheen of pale pink on her lips. She wore a black polo neck tucked into ankle crop blue jeans and I remember thinking straight away that she could model for Attitude with no problem at all, being a bit of a dead ringer for Grace Kelly herself. With looks like that, I imagined Mrs Rodgers, like an ill-behaved dog, biting her hand off!

'Someone hanging about?' asked Jude, frowning. 'What?' He shrugged, a twist to his lips. 'A man?'

'Well, I don't know how to describe this person. Someone who was built like a man, that's for sure. Please sit down. Would you like coffee?'

We both nodded and she went off into the kitchen, leaving Jude and me alone to gaze at our surroundings, everything pristine and in its place. A collection of glass cats and dogs stood on a blonde wood sideboard, together with a record player and a collection of vinyl records, both singles and LPs. Jude wandered over and took a cursory glance at them, thumbing through the singles.

'Hmm, big fan of The Beatles by the look of it.'

'Yeah, no wonder,' I said. 'Their music is fantastic. And so is John Lennon.'

Jude gave me a look of mock jealousy and I laughed. Then, suddenly, a horrible sense of foreboding overcame me at Suzanne's words — *someone built like a man, that's for sure.*

As soon as she came back into the sitting room carrying a tray with coffee percolator, cups and a plate of biscuits, I blurted out, 'Do you know anybody called Dennis Simpson?'

'No.' Frowning, she shook her head and then looking at Jude, asked, 'I hope you approve of my record collection?'

'I'm sorry,' he said, his cheeks tinged pink. 'I shouldn't have looked at your private stuff.'

'Hey, that's fine. Most of them were Mum's anyway, although I do play them. She got me into her music and, yeah, she certainly had a thing about The Beatles, John Lennon in particular. Sugar?' She looked at me, then frowned. 'Wait a minute, though, that name does ring a bell. Dennis Simpson . . .'

'Could you give us a bit more information about this man you've seen hanging about?' asked Jude. 'I only ask because I believe it might have some bearing on your case.'

'Really?' she replied, looking up and almost spilling the coffee. She set the percolator down and handed us both our cups. 'But . . . how?'

Jude and I exchanged glances.

'It's a long story, but it would really help if you could give us some idea of what this person looks like.'

'Well, whoever it is looks really weird, very tall and broad but dressed as a woman, you know. Long dark hair, long dress . . . strange.'

Jude and I exchanged further glances. No doubt he was wondering, just as I was, what the connection was with Suzanne, me and Dennis Simpson. There had to be a reason why he was hanging around her now.

Taking tiny, bird-like sips of the hot coffee, I said, 'But you don't know the name Dennis Simpson?'

She handed us a plate of what had to be home-made biscuits, 'I'm not sure.

I've seen that name, I know I have…'

'Wow,' said Jude through a mouthful. 'If these are home-made, you make fantastic biscuits.'

She laughed and said, 'Thank you. Mum taught me how to bake. We were never short of biscuits, cakes or puddings. I'm surprised I'm not as big as a house.' And then as if a light bulb had gone on in her head, she exclaimed, 'I know! It's the newspaper cuttings I found. That's where I've seen the name.'

'Newspaper cuttings?' asked Jude.

'Yeah, that's what I want to show you.' She shrugged. 'I don't even know why Mum had them or if they will help in finding my sister, but I kept them for you anyway.'

She leaned over the side of her chair and picked up a box from the floor. An old chocolate box, just like the ones Mum used to have for keeping important papers in, the lid depicting a scene of a thatched cottage set in the midst of a flower-filled garden.

'Look, these were hidden away up in

the attic.'

She handed us several cut-out pieces of newspaper that I didn't even need to look at to know what they were. 'They're all about a baby that was taken from his pram, years ago, and the baby's name was Dennis. Not Simpson though, sorry — it's a Mr and Mrs Fishbourne who had their son taken, so he was Dennis Fishbourne.'

I could almost see Jude's brain whirring away in his head and in the split second that it took to exchange glances, we'd made the connection.

11

I went back to the office with Jude, even though he said that I could go home if I wanted to, that I'd had a shock and maybe needed time to be alone to think.

But I refused, saying I'd rather go with him. I needed someone to talk to, to help me put this into perspective.

Because, even though Suzanne's mum had kept newspaper cuttings about the abduction of the baby Dennis Simpson (or his real name, Dennis Fishbourne), it didn't necessarily mean that twenty years later, my mum and dad had adopted me from Suzanne's mum. Although, with Suzanne's sightings of Dennis Simpson — for it was obvious it was him because of the dress and the wig — he must know there was a connection between the two of us.

I gazed around the office, glad that I was here with Jude, feeling reassured by the familiarity of the room, by the warm golden bands of sunshine streaming through the large windows and the bubbling of the kettle as it came to the boil on Jude's little primus stove. Even the sight of my typewriter hidden under its dust cover, piled with folders and papers and tiny tapes to be worked through, didn't make me feel less happy about being here.

My thoughts went back to Suzanne's mum. How had she got the newspaper cuttings anyway? It was front-page news well before her time. Had her own mother kept them for some reason and given them to her as a way of pointing out that she was too young to have a child and, to allow her baby to enjoy a better life, she should give her up to this couple who had no children of their own and could afford to give the baby so much more?

Look, she might have said, pointing at the newspaper article. *Their baby was stolen. You should give your baby to them.*

I imagined Rose's mum somehow contacting poor, childless Mr and Mrs

Fishbourne and putting her proposal to them. I saw them accepting the offer and taking me, Rose Fletcher, as their own and changing my name to Esther Fishbourne.

That must be why no official adoption papers had been found as yet. Maybe it had been done privately . . . secretly.

I remember Mum telling me that I was named after Esther Williams, the fancy swimmer who'd starred in all the old black and white films. She'd told me that I should be proud to have such a name as 'there's not many Esthers about nowadays.'

With a start I thought of my middle name, Rose. Suzanne's mum must have named her child after herself. Did Mum and Dad keep Rose as part of my name especially for her? It all made sense, and pointed more and more to Suzanne being my sister and Dennis Simpson definitely not being my brother.

'How did your mum get on with your . . . nan, grandma, what do you call her?' Jude had asked Suzanne carefully.

'Yeah, Nan. OK, I think, but Nan died when I was only ten so, you know, I was still a kid, and didn't really notice things like that. Grandad died before I was born — he had a heart attack when Mum was fourteen so, when Mum got pregnant, Nan had to handle it all alone.'

Jude nodded and said, 'OK. Do you think she might have been more understanding if she'd had her husband, your grandad, as back-up?'

'Maybe.' She shrugged and then said, 'I don't know, though. Don't forget — getting pregnant at sixteen, out of wedlock, was a pretty big thing back then . . . well, actually it's still a pretty big thing now!'

There was a short silence before she said, 'I remember once Mum and Nan arguing and Mum said something like, 'I'd have kept my baby if you hadn't forced me.' But when they saw me listening, they stopped straight away, so it seems to me that Mum was forced to give Rose up.'

Jude put a cup of coffee on my desk

which I sipped gratefully. Lighting a cigarette, he sat on the edge of his desk, legs straight out in front of him, crossed at the ankles. I still felt a bit shaky and out of sorts and I'm sure Suzanne would be feeling pretty much that way too.

'Esther, look at me,' Jude said, putting the tip of his finger under my chin. I looked up and met his bright blue gaze. 'You did suspect this, didn't you? After what Dennis Simpson said, about being adopted . . .'

I nodded and said, 'Yes. Suzanne must think badly of me but I couldn't take it in properly when we were there in the house with her. I should have been kinder, but I had to get away . . .'

'You were kind — as kind as she was in the circumstances.' He took a deep drag of his cigarette, blowing the smoke over his shoulder, and then took a sip of coffee. 'If what we suspect is true, though, Suzanne is your sister. And she's as lovely as you are . . . there sure is a strong resemblance.'

'Yeah — you didn't tell me just how

much of a resemblance, did you?'

Shaking his head, he said, 'I really didn't see it until you were together. It's not just your looks, it's mannerisms too, the way you move. I can't exactly explain it . . .'

Suddenly the phone rang, cutting in to our conversation, and he picked it up, reverting to his professional manner.

'Jude Dunbar, private investigator.' He listened for a minute or two and then said, 'Yes, that's right. I need police surveillance at fifty-six, Lord Street — Suzanne Fletcher, she's had sightings of Dennis Simpson. Yeah, straight away…' He listened again and said, 'Thanks, I'll come by later.' He stubbed his cigarette into the ash tray on his desk.

'He knows the connection, doesn't he?' I said. 'I bet he knows everything. I don't understand why he took Julie, though. What's she got to do with all this? It doesn't make sense.'

Jude shrugged and stubbed out his cigarette in an ash tray, 'It doesn't have to make sense. He took Julie because she's your friend. He wanted to shake you up and get you prepared for everything that was to follow . . . you being adopted by his parents, knowing who your sister is, your real mother having died . . . he was preparing you for everything, Esther, do you see?'

I nodded. 'At least he's not my brother.' Then, after a moment of thought, 'Although that means that Mum and Dad — Reginald and Mary Fishbourne — weren't really my mum and dad at all . . .'

I kept my head down, not wanting Jude to see the tears brimming into my eyes and running down my cheeks. I pulled a tissue from a box and dabbed at my face.

'Did they make you happy, Esther?'

I sniffed and nodded. 'Yes, of course they did.'

'Well, in that case, they'll always be your mum and dad. You were lucky. Not all parents make their kids happy. Here.' He put a glass in front of me filled with a generous amount of amber liquid. 'Drink that, it'll make you feel better.'

I recognised the smell of brandy from the last time I'd been in shock. It had been when we were in Leopold's just after I'd found out that Mum and Dad's baby had been stolen and they'd not told me anything about it.

I took a large gulp and felt the brandy run through my veins like fire.

'Oh Jude,' I said. 'Do you remember when I said what a tragedy it was that Suzanne's mum had died so young?'

Jude nodded and came to hunker down beside me, his arm around my shoulders.

'I didn't know then, did I, that she was my mum too . . .'

I looked up and into his eyes and Jude smiled at me, his nose almost touching mine.

'Tear-stained and bedraggled, you're still beautiful. I love you, Esther Chambers.'

I gave a tearful grin and squeezing his

hand, said, 'I love you too, Jude Dunbar.'

* * *

'Hey, Tony!' I said, shouting through the door to the kitchens where I could see Tony, Marie and another man I'd never seen before busy cooking. The room was full of steam from pans boiling on the stove top and the spitting and splattering of fried eggs and bacon sizzling in massive frying pans. 'I'm finally all packed and ready to go.'

Tony came over to me, wiping his hands on a blue and white striped apron tied around his waist.

'Esther, sad times, huh?'

He clasped me to him and kissed me wholeheartedly first on one cheek and then the other, giving great smacking sounds as he did so. He smelled oily, of onions and garlic.

Jude, coming down the stairs carrying a cardboard box said, 'Hey Tony, not so many kisses, OK? She's my girl.'

'Jude!' he replied, throwing up his hands. 'You take her away from here, you better look after her good.'

Jude laughed, throwing back his head, as he walked on out to the car.

I smiled as I noticed that the box he carried contained all the most important things, like the kettle and cups, coffee and sugar, even the book I had now almost finished reading, *In Cold Blood* by Truman Capote, sticking out at the top.

A wall of heat hit me as I walked outside, squinting into the sunshine. There were plenty of people wandering about the streets because of the fine day, and a lot of customers in The Milk Maid drinking coffee and chatting to one another as they waited for their cooked breakfasts.

'Do you have that record on repeat?' I asked Tony, as I heard again the strains of the Moody Blues singing *Go Now*, streaming from the open doorway of the café. 'Are you trying to tell me something?'

He laughed and, lightly squeezing my shoulder said simply, 'Keep in touch,

Esther.'

Jude put the box in the boot and, as we pulled away from the kerb, tooted the horn loud enough for all the street to hear. I waved through the open window as Tony raised his hand and then turning around, he went back inside and was soon swallowed up by the dark hole of the doorway.

* * *

The communal gardens were bathed in sunshine, all the trees and flowers shining deep greens, reds, pinks and blues, and shimmering in the heat.

Jude and I, joined by Martha, who had come to wish me well in my new home, were sitting on the balcony enjoying the warmth of the sun, and drinking fizzy champagne from long tall glasses. Martha looked summery in a short-sleeved flower-patterned dress, calf length and belted in tight at her dumpy waist. She had her iron-grey hair pulled back tight from her face and tiny earrings shone from her ears. She'd arrived almost hidden behind an enormous bouquet of fragrant pink roses.

Taking a tentative sip, I said, 'Is this stuff stronger than Babycham?'

I was aware that Jude and Martha exchanged amused glasses. Jude said, 'Um . . . yeah, I should say so.'

Martha laughed. 'Yeah — watch your head, Esther baby, or it might explode.' She took a grateful sip and licked her lips. 'This is good stuff . . . cheers.' She raised her glass. 'And be happy in your new home.'

'Thanks, Martha. I'm sure I will. I was happy at The Milk Maid until all this stuff with Dennis Simpson.'

Jude moved closer and put a protective arm around my shoulders.

'Yeah, things have a funny way of working out. If I hadn't met you all this stuff with Dennis Simpson and Julie might never have happened, and my job of finding Suzanne's sister would have been a lot more difficult.'

'Well, if you really want to go down

that road, you can blame your Aunt Maud. She brought you to Attitude and asked for me to model in the first place.'

Jude laughed, his baby blues sparkling with mirth.

'Yeah, and ain't that right,' said Martha. 'I remember the day well.'

'Yeah, so do I,' agreed Jude.

There was a short silence as we sipped our drinks, enjoying the bubbles popping in our mouths and up our noses. The sun shone even warmer and bees buzzed languidly around the flowers.

'So,' said Martha giving me a sidelong glance. 'This Suzanne, she's your sister, right?'

'Yeah,' I said, giving a wry smile. 'Everything seems to point to it at the moment, doesn't it, Jude?'

'Yeah, it does . . . and there's definitely a resemblance.' He got up and went to lean against the balcony railings, legs crossed at the ankles. He opened a pack of cigarettes and lit up.

'What? Two Grace Kelly lookalikes?' said Martha in mock surprise, putting her hands to her cheeks. 'I sure would love to see that, and if she looks like you, wouldn't Mrs Rodgers just love her at Attitude?'

I nodded, 'I thought that too. But she's got a good job, she's a legal secretary. Boy, am I still trying to get my head round the situation, Martha, and I'm sure Suzanne feels the same way. I feel really overwhelmed at the moment.'

'Yeah, yeah,' Martha replied, gently patting my arm. 'Things will soon start to make sense, Esther baby, just you wait and see.' And then she changed the subject. 'You been to Attitude to show the girls your ring?'

Spreading my hand out in front of me so the ring twinkled in the sunlight, I smiled and said, 'No, I haven't yet . . .'

'Oh you need to, Esther baby, you gotta flaunt it. Pam especially will be pea green with envy.'

I thought about Martha's words later as I sat alone in my new flat, Martha having gone home and Jude out for a meeting with a client. I truly hoped that things would make sense soon too but at the moment I was finding it hard to come to terms with.

I know it's a terrible cliché, but I'd lost sight of myself. I didn't know who I was. My parents weren't really my parents and I felt lost and alone, adrift, with nothing to hold me down, like I could fly away at any time like a helium filled balloon.

I remembered Marty Valesko telling us that Dennis Simpson had said that very thing to him when he found out that his parents weren't who he thought they were. It must be a common way to feel in the circumstances and, as much as I knew Suzanne had been through the mangle too, I couldn't connect with her yet. It was too soon.

It was very quiet here, and in a way I missed the thump thump from the jukebox in The Milk Maid and the chattering of customers, even the shouting backwards and forwards of Tony and Marie in the kitchens. No doubt I would get used to it in time.

Gazing around at boxes piled up everywhere, I roused myself from the effects of the champagne and started to unpack all the kitchen equipment.

I stood the kettle on the stove top, put cups and plates into one of the many cupboards and slotted knives and forks into the cutlery drawer.

Immersed in such mundane tasks, I almost jumped out of my skin at the ringing of the telephone. Running into the bedroom, I stared at it for a minute or two, that great black hulking thing sitting on the bedside cabinet, as if it was something gruesome from a horror film, before gingerly picking up the receiver and saying, 'Hello?'

A voice just as hesitant as mine said, 'Hi . . . it's Suzanne.'

I'd given her my new number just in case anything turned up, like a sighting of Dennis Simpson, or she just simply wanted to talk. She sounded very young, much younger than eighteen, like a small child.

My heart did a little leap as I said,

'Suzanne, hello, how are you?'

'Esther, I've found some letters that I think will be of interest to you . . . and to Jude.'

'OK . . . that's good. I thought you were going to say that there'd been a sighting of Dennis Simpson.'

'No, there's been no sign of him. But I've found letters from Nan to Mr and Mrs Fishbourne and vice versa . . .'

I felt a pang at the casual way she said Mr and Mrs Fishbourne

'Well, Jude isn't here at the moment but I'll tell him about them when he gets back.'

'You're welcome to call round, Esther — alone, I mean. I can't wait for you to read the letters. Do we have to wait for Jude?'

I hesitated, not knowing whether it was the right thing to do — but, hey, I reasoned, I was Jude's assistant and this was work after all, however much of a personal element there was.

'OK . . . give me half an hour. Jude said he'll call here before going back to his place, so I'll leave a note for him to call at yours.'

She agreed so I hurried into the bathroom to freshen up, hoping that my outfit of a white embroidered peasant blouse tucked into blue jeans was smart enough.

I scribbled a note telling Jude where I'd gone and, stepping around all the boxes that I really should be unpacking, I grabbed a jacket and my bag. Picking up the key, I locked the door behind me and left the flat to visit Suzanne.

12

By the time I got to Suzanne's house, dark clouds were edging in, blocking out the sun and spits and spots of rain had begun to fall. I knocked on the door, my denim jacket draped over my head like an umbrella.

I'd been in such a rush to go out that I'd forgotten to bring a scarf, gloves or even a hat. I hadn't expected to need them — it had been so hot earlier.

I noticed the police car still parked discreetly at the kerb. Two different police officers by the look of it and not the usual ones, Laurel and Hardy, as Jude called them. Vigilant ones this time, I hoped.

Suzanne opened the door laughing at my bedraggled state and, once inside, handed me a towel for the raindrops that dripped from my hair onto the hallway floor. A Beatles album spun around on the record player, John Lennon and Paul

McCartney singing in harmony, *That boy took my love away, though he'll regret it someday, but this boy wants you back again . . .*

I followed her into the kitchen where she was making coffee, spooning grounds into the percolator before setting it on the stove top. Peering from the window I saw that there was a small garden at the back with a pocket-sized lawn and colourful flowers and bushes in the borders, all surrounded by a high stone wall.

'Have you always lived here?' I asked her.

'Yeah, I grew up here with Mum . . . and Dad for my first two years but I don't remember that.' The percolator started to bubble gently so Suzanne busied herself with getting cups from the cupboard and setting them on the worktop. She glanced at me from the corner of her eye as she said, 'It must have been dreadful when you lost your mum and dad?'

Oh, and this boy would be happy, just to love you but oh my, that boy won't be happy, til he's seen you cry . . .

I nodded. 'Yeah. You know it was a car accident, don't you?'

'Yeah, my mum saw it in the paper. She obviously had some idea of who had adopted you because I remember her being upset. I didn't know about you then. Even when Mum did finally tell me I had an adopted sister, there was no detail, just your name, Rose Fletcher. That's all I had to go on.'

We went into the sitting room, Suzanne carrying the tea tray. She'd lit the fire and it roared up the chimney behind the fireguard, its flames yellow, orange and red. The weather had changed beyond all recognition from this morning. Rain was coming down heavily now, bouncing onto the pavements in long silver sheets, and a strong wind howled around the house like ghosts.

Clutching my coffee cup in two hands, I hunched nearer to the fire, and took a sip of the fragrant brew.

'Mm, you make fantastic coffee.'

She took a sip of hers and said, 'Yeah, it's really good percolated.' Putting her cup down on the coffee table, she picked up a similar looking box to the one she'd had last time, an old chocolate box with a pretty scene on the lid, and opened it. 'I found this hidden away right at the back of a drawer in the sideboard. Mum obviously wanted me to find it eventually, otherwise she'd have thrown it all away, wouldn't she?'

I shrugged. 'Maybe . . . yeah . . .' And then, 'Why do you think your mum didn't try to find me?'

'I think because of Nan. If she'd died, Mum wouldn't have hesitated . . . actually, the only reason I've felt OK to contact you is because my Nan doesn't know.'

'Is your Nan still alive?' Suzanne had told Jude that her nan — well, possibly my nan too — had died when she was ten.

'Yeah, but she's in a nursing home, she's gone senile. So I'm free to do as I please. Look . . .' She handed me a letter written on ordinary white lined paper inside an ordinary white envelope, post-marked the twenty-second of December, 1943.

'My birthday's on the ninth,' I exclaimed. 'I was about two weeks old.'

Dear Mrs Fletcher,

Thank you for your letter received 24th December.

My husband and I have a very great interest in your granddaughter, Rose. We suffered a terrible trauma when our baby son, Dennis, was stolen from his pram so many years ago now, and in that intervening time, he's never been found and we've never been blessed by another child. The letter received from you was like the answer to a prayer. We will give this child, Rose, all the things that you can't give her at this time — security, stability, love and so much more.

Please write by return so that we may have her in our arms as soon as it can be arranged.

Yours sincerely
Mr and Mrs Reginald Fishbourne

My first thought was that I'd guessed this had happened, I'd suspected a private adoption. But, shaking my head in total disbelief at the contents of the letter, I said, 'Obviously your nan wrote to them?'

Suzanne nodded. 'Yes, she did. It's awful, isn't it? It doesn't look as if Mum had any say in the matter.'

'How did your nan know where they lived?'

'I've no idea,' replied Suzanne.

'Hmm,' I said, shaking my head. 'My mum always said I was the best Christmas present she ever had.' I looked at Suzanne. 'It wasn't just because I was born near Christmas, as I thought it was, but because I was adopted at Christmas too . . .' I gave a little laugh. 'You learn something new every day, don't you?'

Suzanne gave a small smile.

'Maybe they were planning on telling you when you got older . . . maybe twenty-one?'

I nodded.'Yeah, that's what Jude says.'

'The newspaper cuttings are still a bit of a mystery though, aren't they?'

'Yeah . . . your nan couldn't see into the future. She didn't know that one day her daughter would get pregnant and they'd need somebody to adopt the baby, did she?'

Suzanne smiled.

'Maybe she just had an interest in the case. Thinking about it, I know some-one at work who keeps all the newspaper cuttings about the Moors Murders!'

'Oh no . . . that's creepy!'

'It's quite common though.'

I rifled through the rest of the letters, reading through little bits here and there. Suzanne's nan had written back within a day arranging a time for them to meet with the baby and arrange a handover. It was difficult to come to terms with the fact that the baby they were talking about was me.

I read the section of the letter about security, stability and love to Suzanne who said wryly, 'Yeah — for some rea-son, no one at all thought that a sixteen-year-old could give all those things to her own child. It's all very sad, and Nan could have helped her. I wish you'd met my mum . . . just for a minute . . . a second even . . .'

Suzanne's eyes filled with tears that threatened to fall. She dabbed at them with her fingertips.

'So do I,' I said, leaning forward and patting her on the shoulder.

Suddenly there was a great blaze of blue light that lit up the room and a deafening crack of thunder. Then the rain, even heavier than before, hit the ground like bullets. The room was very dark now, with just the glow from the fire.

We'd been so immersed in the letters that we hadn't noticed the Beatles record coming to an end and it still spun around on the turntable, the needle scratching on the vinyl. Quickly Suzanne jumped up and removed the needle so there was a deep dark silence.

It was broken suddenly by a tapping on the window, making us jump violently.

We both rushed to look out, pulling the curtain fully back, but could barely see anything in the gloom except the swaying and dancing of trees in the strong wind. Backing away from the window, afraid that it was Dennis Simpson standing there and staring at me with his dead eyes, we jumped again as there was a loud banging on the door and a voice called, 'Esther! Suzanne! Let me in. It's raining like crazy out here.'

My hands to my heart, I said with relief, 'It's OK, it's Jude,' and ran to the door to let him in.

He came in, seeming larger than life in the tiny hallway, shaking the rain from his coat like a wet dog. His eyes sparkled very blue and it took all my self-control not to fling myself into his arms and nestle into him purring like a pet cat but I really didn't like to do that in front of Suzanne.

'Wow,' he said, 'What a change in the weather. I tapped on the window but you couldn't hear me.'

'Oh, so it was you scaring us half to

death! With the thunder and lightning too, it was terrifying.'

'Hey, were you both spooked?'

We nodded as Suzanne poured him coffee which he gulped thankfully. I showed him the letters, telling him that it looked without a doubt that I had been adopted by the Fishbournes and it had been done privately. That was obviously why there were no official adoption papers.

He picked up some of the letters and scanned through them, shaking his head and glancing at me and Suzanne from time to time.

'These are terrible, but I'm glad they've been found. How do you two feel about them?'

I gave a little laugh and said, 'It's almost like I was sold at market . . . you know, auctioned off to the highest bidder.'

'I just think it's sad that Esther and I missed out on so many years of being sisters,' said Suzanne. And then, 'Oh, I found a photo . . . my mum and baby

Rose just before the adoption. I'm surprised it exists. Mum hated being photographed.'

Jude and I took the little square black and white photo from Suzanne's fingers and bent forward peering greedily.

Jude smiled and said, 'Wow, Esther baby, you're a clone of your mum. And you too, Suzanne.'

I gazed at the picture feeling sad, knowing that whatever happened I'd never be able to speak to the woman in the picture, or spend time with her as Suzanne had. But then again I'd been lucky enough to grow up with a lovely mum too.

Oh, my head felt as if it was spinning with all the information that it had taken in lately. Jude's voice broke into my thoughts.

'Well, you two have a lot of catching up to do — as I have, work-wise. I need to get back to the office.'

'Yeah, I'll go back with you. I've work to do too. The last time I was in the office, I couldn't see my typewriter for all the files and tapes it was buried under.'

'You can borrow these if you like,' said Suzanne, handing over the box. 'Read them at your leisure and bring them back next time you visit.'

I gave her the photo back but she said, 'No — you keep that, Esther.'

I took the box and the photo with a smile and we hugged before Jude and I went out to the car. Unbelievably the rain had stopped now and the sun shone again in a blue sky speckled with cloud. The air felt warm and heavy as if we waded through treacle.

Suzanne waved and, as the car pulled away, I raised my hand and watched her until, gradually growing smaller and smaller, she became a tiny dot and then quite suddenly disappeared from view.

* * *

'Esther, you're not going to like this,' said Jude. He was prowling up and down the office as if he just couldn't bear to sit still. He wore a black suit with a white shirt, the top buttons of which were undone showing a mat of chest hair amidst which hung a gold cross on a slim link chain. He hadn't taken off his hat, a trilby that he'd pushed to the back of his head so that he bore a marked resemblance to a very cute Frank Sinatra or Dean Martin. A bright shaft of sunlight shone through the window, pooling onto the carpet in a yellow glow.

'What's wrong?' I asked, raising my eyes but not fully listening as I was sitting at my desk, rifling through all the files and papers, trying to make sense of the work that I needed to do. There was a Mr Lund who suspected his wife of an affair with his brother; a Mrs Crowther whose husband had gone missing; he hadn't been seen for two weeks now and she was starting to get worried (*starting* to get worried?).

I had pages of scribbled notes to be typed up and a lot of little tapes containing letters to be sent out and there were documents to be copied. I could see that a busy afternoon awaited me. I must have been dreaming to think I could take today off to move in! Modelling was a doddle compared to this!

'Esther?' Jude had hunkered down by my side, his hand cupping my shoulder. 'Listen to me . . .'

I gazed straight into his baby blue eyes.

'What, Jude? Is this urgent? Look how busy I am! There's so much to do.'

'Yeah, I know, but it's urgent all right. I've been to the court to get a copy of the Decree Absolute.'

'Yeah? Oh, that's good. Can we set a date soon, then?'

'From the divorce . . . you know?'

'I know what a Decree Absolute is, Jude!'

He gave a small smile.

'I know you do. That's not what I'm saying.'

'Well, did you get it?'

'Well, that's what I'm trying to tell you, Esther . . . no.'

'Well, where is it, then?'

'I don't know . . . to tell you the honest truth, Esther, there's no record of it at all.'

The enormity of what he was trying to tell me suddenly sank in and, giving him my full attention, I said, 'You mean there isn't one?'

He stood up and, putting his hands in his pockets, moved away and stood gazing from one of the beautiful arched windows that looked out onto the street.

'I don't think she ever lodged one. I really can't believe it.'

Very faintly I could hear traffic outside on the busy road, the squeak of vehicles pulling up at the kerb, the squeal of tyres, the beeping of horns, people talking and shouting, laughing.

I went to stand behind him, my hand on his shoulder. 'You mean, you're not divorced?'

He turned and pulled me in close to him, sadly shaking his head.

'Esther, I don't think I am...' His mouth found my neck and he kissed it and breathed in deeply, 'Youth Dew, huh?'

With tears pricking at the back of my eyelids and a touch of hysteria in my voice, I said, 'So we can't get married?'

'Not yet,' he said, pulling back from me a little and gazing at my face with those sparkly baby blues, 'Esther . . . I'm going to have go over the pond as they say to track her down and get this sorted.'

'What? No, you can't, Jude!' I pulled away from him and backed off, my arms crossed over my breasts. He fumbled in his pocket and took out a pack of cigarettes. With a shaky hand, he put one in his mouth, lit it and took a deep drag.

'I'll have to. If I don't get the Decree Absolute, there will be no wedding and, Esther, believe me, I want to marry you.'

'How come there isn't one? What happened?'

'I don't know.' He raised his hands, the cigarette glowing brightly between his fingers. 'She, Myra that is, told me that she put in for it after we got the Decree Nisi and that it was lodged at the Court House right here in London. That was ages ago, at least four years now.'

Smoke billowed from his mouth as he spoke.

'Four years? Oh, Jude! Maybe she has it with her in America?'

He shrugged and shook his head.

'If it existed, I'd be able to get a copy.'

'Can't you just phone her somehow? Why do you have to go all that way?'

'Esther baby, I haven't got a phone number for her. I'm not even sure if I've got an up-to-date address! It's a great big wide world out there and she's in America! But I'll track her down somehow . . . oh, I will . . .'

In that instant, he looked both mean and crazy, and not like Jude at all. I was mightily glad he wasn't trailing me all the way to America, that's for sure!

'I wondered why you were so quiet in the car after leaving Suzanne's.'

He gave a watery grin.

'Yeah, I was wrestling with how I was gonna tell you about it. After all, you've been through lately, this was just another nail in the coffin.'

'It is the truth, isn't it, Jude? You're

not saying this because you don't want us to get married?'

'No, of course not! I want to marry you, without a doubt.'

'Is Myra the one who used to wear Youth Dew?' I asked quietly.

'What? No. Why do you ask that?'

'Well, when you first smelled it on me, you mentioned that you recognised it from somewhere.'

'I've only ever smelled it on you. I meant that I recognised it from the shops. Women spray perfumes around in chemists before they buy.'

I sat down at my desk, putting my head in my hands. He hunkered down beside me again and put his an arm around my shoulders.

'Oh, Esther. Look, don't worry, I'll sort this out and before you know it, you'll be Mrs Esther Dunbar. I promise you that.' Tenderly he kissed the little scar just above my lip. 'Although, thinking about it, Esther Chambers sounds better . . . it's got more of a ring to it.'

We both giggled, amid the tears running down my cheeks, wetting Jude's, making him put a hand to his cheek and say in mock jest, 'Hey, what's going on, where's all this water coming from? Are you leaking?'

I turned my face up to him and his mouth met mine and stayed there, and stayed there . . . if the telephone hadn't rung, the shrill sound cutting through the air and disturbing us, I think his mouth would still be on mine now. Although, from what happened next, perhaps not.

He picked up the receiver cutting off the ringing.

'Jude Dunbar!'

He listened for a second and frowning, said, 'Yeah, she's here, I'll pass you over...'

I took the receiver from his hand, 'Hello?'

'Hi, Esther baby, guess who?'

My heart lurched as if it would come up out of my throat.

'What do you want?'

'What do you think I want?'

Jude was looking at me confused and mouthing, 'Who is it?'

I ignored him and concentrated instead on the phone call,

'I think you want money . . . Dennis Simpson!'

Jude mouthed, 'No, Esther . . . no!' He looked pained as he put the palm of his hand to his head.

I put up a warning hand as I listened to Dennis Simpson's demands.

'OK,' I said. 'I'll be there with the money at the phone box near Attitude Boutique on Carnaby Street.'

'It better be tomorrow, Esther baby.'

'No — how do you think I can get that sort of money by tomorrow? It'll have to be four or five days at least.'

'OK, Friday then. That gives you almost a week. You better be there, or I'll take Julie again.'

'Hey, you leave Julie alone. I can get it by Friday, I'll be there.'

My hands shaking and my palms wet with sweat, I hung up the receiver.

'Wow, I didn't recognise his voice'

said Jude. 'Otherwise I'd have got rid of him.' And then as if thinking aloud, 'What we'll have to do is get the police there, then when he turns up, we'll nab him, haul him in and you take your money back.'

'No Jude, I don't care about the money. I want to deal with this my way!'

'Esther . . .'

'If I give him the money, he'll disappear and be gone forever. If he doesn't get it, he said he'd take Julie again . . .'

'He won't get anywhere near Julie, we won't let him, and he'll be back for more money — that's the way these people work, Esther, believe me, I've seen this before.'

'No, I'll give him enough that he won't need to come back.'

'He's a wanted man, you'd be breaking the law if you do this.'

'No . . . I'm doing it my way. With or without you.'

A sudden hot wave of anger overcame me and before I knew what I was doing, I took my beautiful engagement ring from my finger and set it down on Jude's desk.

'Here, you can have this back, Jude, you can't marry me anyway. You say 'not yet' but it'll probably be 'never'!'

Wrestling into my jacket and pulling my bag onto my shoulder, I stalked to the door. I remembered the box of letters and picked those up too.

Jude, as if in a state of shock, stared at me, his usually glittering blue eyes, blank and lifeless.

'You can't be serious, Esther. We can't let this come between us.'

He picked up the ring and put out an arm to stop me from walking out of the door.

'Put the ring back on . . . please . . . it's your engagement ring, we're gonna be married, Esther!'

'Don't touch me,' I said, putting up a hand. 'I'm doing this my way, Jude.' However hard I tried to suppress them, tears threatened. 'I should have known you wouldn't be on my side!'

Before I really did break down and

cry, I barged out of the door and ran down the steps and out into the warm afternoon sunshine. I could hear Jude calling after me, 'Esther! Esther . . . you can't be serious . . .'

13

Putting the last of the money into the leather case, I snapped it shut and gazed at it with satisfaction. Everything from the sale of the house was in that case, every beautiful crisp note of it!

I was pretty skint now so without a doubt I'd have to go back to Attitude to earn a living because I certainly couldn't be Jude's assistant any more, I'd pushed that job well and truly out of the window.

A shame really, because I'd certainly enjoyed the excitement of it and being with Jude every day had been a wonderful added bonus.

I hadn't handed in my notice as yet though, but left him an answerphone message at the office pleading sickness. He could make of that whatever he wanted. I really didn't care at the moment.

I knew that Mrs Rodgers would welcome me back, after all she'd told me she would time and time again, and I knew that Julie and Jane would too. Pam was another problem altogether, but hey, maybe she'd be gone by now. Maybe some rich guy had taken her away with promises of marriage and a better life.

Huh . . . knowing Pam though she wouldn't be as gullible as I'd been and would tell him to go hoot.

That expression made me think of Martha and I promised myself that, after I'd got this business with Dennis Simpson over and done with, I'd go see her and persuade her to go back to Attitude with me. We'd made a great team before, so no doubt we would again.

I hadn't heard from Jude, despite leaving him the message about being sick, and I was really doing my best to not want him but, hey, come on, give me a break, he's the cutest man in shoe leather and it was really difficult to stop myself from phoning or giving in by telling him I'll go along with whatever he wants regarding Dennis Simpson.

But I can't . . . I really can't. I can't back down now, after all I'm all set and ready to go with the money. All I need to do is leave the case in the phone box and go. Easy . . . right?

We'd said midday, a good time because there'd be loads of people about, and I can mingle in amongst the crowds, especially today as it was warm and sunny.

There were hardly any clouds, just a few white skeins floating around like leftover wool and the air smelled fresh and clean, with just a hint of cooked pizza and percolating coffee from nearby cafés.

There was a strong hoppy smell of beer sneaking out from the open doors of pubs and the fresh green smell of cut grass as people got to work in their gardens, mowing and cutting like crazy.

I felt nervous and shaky as if everyone was looking at me, and knew exactly what I was doing, that somehow they knew I was carrying a case full of money.

I reached Carnaby Street and tried to

be casual, sauntering along, peering in at the window of Attitude to have a look at the clothes, comparing the window display with London Girl and a few other ladies clothes shops like Roxette that have live models posing in the windows wearing underwear and skimpy bathing suits.

It seemed to be getting warmer and the case even more heavy and uncomfortable, but it wouldn't be long now and I'd be able to dispose of it. Just a few more minutes, just until I get into the phone box.

Damn, there was someone in there, someone casually leaning against the glass and talking on the phone . . . oh my God, I hoped they were quick. Luckily there wasn't a queue. Glancing at my little Ingersoll watch, I saw that it was a couple of minutes to twelve so it was OK . . . everything was fine at the moment. I wasn't late.

I was sweating though, under my arms, the back of my neck, even the back of my knees feel as though they're running with perspiration. My scalp is itchy and my mouth dry and my heart's clattering away nearly as hard as it did the first time I ever set eyes on Jude Dunbar.

Glancing around, my eyes skittering in their sockets, I couldn't see any police; they must be under cover. Jude would, without a doubt, have told them when it was going to happen. I should have confused him and changed the day but didn't know how to get in touch with Dennis Simpson.

Hopefully Dennis would grab the suitcase and run like hell. My heart was beating faster, it was a minute to twelve and the person was still on the phone.

Please hurry, hurry. What are they talking about? Hurry, hurry.

I felt someone pushing close behind me, breathing heavily. I saw a flash of red from the corner of my eye. People are flowing around me on the busy street like water around rocks. My heartbeat slowed down a bit as I saw the person in the phone box finish their conversation and hang up. Then they were holding the door open, holding it wide so I could go in. I took the door with a shaky hand and a nod of thanks. I step inside, put the case down on the floor.

The phone box smelled of stale cigarettes and, beneath my feet, dog ends floated in little pools of water. I recoiled at having to pick up the black Bakelite receiver that looks wet, with the imprint of the other person's hand clearly visible, but I do, and press it to my ear.

I pretended to press a coin into the slot, to talk, to laugh. And then I hung up and held the door for the next person, who sidled in. I caught a glimpse of long red hair, a black outfit as they brushed past me. *It must be him . . .*

I heard a shout as, legs trembling, I hurried away, glancing quickly over my shoulder to see the person with red hair surrounded by uniforms, police cars at the kerb, lights flashing. Quickly I scanned all the faces, but I couldn't see Jude's.

Panic struck, I knew that I'd failed.

Dennis Simpson (with red hair this time?) wouldn't be getting his money — and, worse than that, probably thought that I'd stitched him up.

I went into a café and, sitting at a table near the window, ordered a coffee. It was weak and watery, tasteless but so boiling hot it burned my mouth.

Jude obviously alerted the police, which I know was the right thing to do, but if Dennis Simpson ever got out again, he'd come after me until he got the money. I may never be free of him.

That's what Jude couldn't understand, that in some weird way I felt responsible for Dennis Simpson, as if I really did take the life that he should have had and that the money from my Mum and Dad's house really did belong to him and not to me. I was just the adopted daughter whereas he, as Dennis Simpson himself had said, was the true born child . . . the stolen baby. The poor, defenceless stolen baby.

Feeling down and disheartened I walked slowly home, totally unaware of the crowds of people milling about on the streets, locked in my own little world, wishing in some ways that I was going back to my little flat above the The Milk Maid, to Tony and Marie, the chattering customers, even the muscular guy who delivered the bread, and even the thump thump of the jukebox.

Sadly I swung through the ornate revolving door at Richmond Villas, my head hanging and my mouth in a downturn, and make my way up the stairs all the way to the third floor, my thighs tingling by the time I got to the top. There were two square white envelopes on the door mat addressed to me. I recognised Jude's handwriting straight away.

Sitting on the balcony, the afternoon sunshine warm on my skin, I tore one of the envelopes open and, smoothing the letter out on my lap, began to read . . .

My darling Esther,

I'm imagining you reading this letter, maybe sitting on your balcony in the afternoon sun, maybe sitting in a café drinking coffee or maybe even in the office, surrounded by your typewriter and papers, but wherever you are, I see your face, your beautiful face and know that what I'm about to do is the right thing.

Yes . . . going 'across the pond' (what pond? I remember you saying) to track down my ex and get my Decree Absolute is absolutely (no pun intended) the right thing to do . . . because without that I can't marry you and my life will have no meaning, Esther baby, if I can't spend the rest of it with you as my wife.

I'm sorry about today but Dennis Simpson had to be caught, he had to pay for putting Julie through hell and for attempting to do the same to you. If we hadn't got him today and put him behind bars, he would have stalked you all your life. However much money you threw at him, he'd have been back for more. Well, Esther, we've got him now and you are FREE! Yeah . . . capital letters FREE! He won't escape again. There's no chance of that. And he'll be given a longer sentence because of the escape.

Your money is safe and in the post office on Lombard Street, PO Box number 69712. The key for that box is enclosed in the other envelope that I posted through your door.

My work is being looked after by an old pal of mine called Buddy Lewis. I've given him your contact number at the office so he might get in touch for help with admin.

I know you're angry with me at the moment but please, Esther, wait for me. I'll be back as soon I can with the Decree Absolute, but remember that I love you and won't let you down.

Jude x

Tears burning at the back of my eyes, I tore open the other envelope and let the contents drop into my lap.

There was a tiny silver key and, falling on top of it with a chink, something that sparkled brightly in the sunshine.

Gently I picked up my engagement ring, toying with it for a moment or two, before putting it back into the envelope. I didn't feel ready for it to go back on my finger just yet.

Overwhelmed with a sudden grief, I put my face in my hands and wept.

* * *

'Hey, Esther baby! Open up.' Bang, bang, bang on the door. 'Esther baby! Hey, come on. It's me, Martha.'

I came up out of what felt like a swamp, as if I'd been somewhere heavy and dark and was coming up into the light, like one of those weird sea creatures that live right down deep on the bed of the ocean.

I thought the banging was in my head, after an evening of too many of those sweet delicious Babychams, but it was the door. Someone knocking on the door.

Pulling myself out of bed, I shrugged on a dressing gown and pushing my feet into mules, stumbled out of the bedroom and flung open the door.

Martha flew in like a whirlwind.

'Oh, Esther baby, you're here and OK. I was worried about you.' She looked at her wrist watch and shrugging, palms up, exclaimed, 'Eleven o'clock and you're still in your robe!'

I put a hand to my head as I closed the door and said, 'Oh Martha, please . . .'

'Hey, I'm sorry, Esther baby. I'll put the kettle on.' She hung her coat on the stand and bustled into the kitchen. 'Sit down,' she shouted, 'I'll bring it in.'

The percolator bubbled and the smell of fresh coffee streamed through the air. I heard the soft thunk of the fridge door and the soft opening and closing of cupboards and drawers before Martha walked in carrying a tray.

I sat on the settee, clutching my coffee cup in both hands, inhaling the lovely aroma. I took a sip and the smooth liquid made its luxurious way down my throat and into my stomach. I sat back, leaning my head against the cushions, breathing deeply.

'Make you feel better, huh?' said Martha with a smile.

I nodded my thanks and she said, 'I'm sorry for barging in like that, Esther baby, but when you didn't answer the door earlier, or the phone, I got worried.'

'Oh, I'm sorry, I didn't hear you earlier. I didn't hear the phone ring either! I was deep in dreams.'

She gave me a harsh glare.

'You ain't been drinking that Babycham stuff, have you?'

'No! . . .'

'Hmm. I knew you'd be feeling down with him gone and all.'

I perked up immediately and gave her a stare.

'You mean Jude? How d'you know he's gone?'

She gave me a sly grin.

'You ain't the only woman gets letters from a good looking man you know, Esther baby. Yeah, he wrote to me too!'

'Well . . . how dare he!'

'He loves you . . . and I'd be seeing you anyway. He wants to make sure you're OK while he's gone, and here when he gets back . . . hmm, hmm.'

Restlessly I got up and peered from the window. I saw a hard blue sky with only tiny fragments of cloud and the sun pulsing like a fried egg in a pan.

'Hey, it looks as if it's a nice day out there, Martha. Let's go sit on the balcony.'

The room felt stuffy so I cranked open the window and breathed in the air that came pouring in — along with the sounds of cars rushing past, horns blaring and people laughing and shouting.

'You go bathe first and get dressed. Do you want everyone to see you with just your robe on?' She gave me another harsh glare as, laughing and shaking my head, I sauntered off towards the bathroom.

'OK,' I shouted back to her. 'As long as you come with me to Attitude today . . .'

She followed me and stood in the doorway as I ran water and bath oil into the tub and churned it up with my hand until big bouncy bubbles floated around the room.

'Well, Esther baby, I'm not sure, seeing as I'm at London Girl now . . .' pushed a particularly large bubble towards Martha and giggled as it popped into tiny drops of water in her hair. The sharp heady smell of lavender hung in the air.

'Oh . . . so you don't want to come back with me to Attitude?'

'Well, I suppose I could go along,' she said as if she didn't care either way, even though I knew she did. 'See what Mrs Rodgers says. What about your job with Jude? Don't you wanna be a private eye no more?'

Pushing the door to, I sank into the bath, immersing myself right up to my neck. Martha would go up ape at the amount of water.

'I'm his assistant, Martha . . . and he's not here . . . and I need money. My own hard-earned money, and not money that Jude might deposit in my bank account.'

Shouting through the door, she said, 'Hey, you can go get your money back from the PO Box . . .'

'So he told you about that too!'

'Yeah, and he was right. Why give away all your money to a deadbeat like

Dennis Simpson, huh?'

'Too many reasons to talk about at the moment, Martha.' Reluctantly I stepped out of the bath and began rubbing myself dry with a fluffy towel.

'Huh, you can tell me all those reasons on the way to Attitude. Hurry up, Esther baby, we need to make Mrs Rodgers' day.'

* * *

I told Martha about the letters that Suzanne had given me to read as we walked through the hot, pungent streets to Attitude. Everything seemed slow and lethargic in the heat, even the leaves on the trees drooped pale and languid and the grass, brown at the edges, looked almost dead.

'You see, Martha, I feel that the money should be Dennis Simpson's because he's their true born son and I'm just an adopted daughter.'

'No.' She shook her head emphatically. 'It don't work like that, Esther baby. Your parents, Mr and Mrs Fishbourne, didn't know Dennis Simpson as their own fully grown son. He was stolen as a baby — now that was a tragedy. But you grew up with them . . . they knew you . . . you were their daughter, adopted or not, so the money is yours! They left it to you in their will, didn't they?'

'They did, but they'd have left it to Dennis if he hadn't been stolen, wouldn't they?'

Martha, puzzled, shook her head. 'This is pure conjecture, Esther baby. They wouldn't have had you if Dennis hadn't been taken. You could go on and on saying stuff like that.'

Stubbornly, I said, 'It's not his fault he was stolen, was it?'

'Oh, and not his fault either that he grew up bad and kidnapped Julie and stalked you? Huh?'

'Oh Martha, we could talk about this until the cows come home, and never agree.'

'Esther baby, we ain't talking about cows,' she said with a frown. 'That an

English saying?' She stopped on the pavement, people moaning and grumbling as they walked around her.

Laughing, I said, 'Yeah, I think it is. Come on, we're here now. Let's go see Mrs Rodgers.'

'Hey, Esther baby, wait a minute.' She pulled at the sleeve of my blouse. 'I'm only going back if you do . . . OK? You hear me?'

'Yes, of course, Martha. I'm not going anywhere without you.'

Crowds of people were congregated on Carnaby Street, both girls and boys preening like peacocks and flirting madly, all trying to outdo each other by wearing fantastic eye-catching outfits of mini skirts with knee-high boots, tight-tting flared jeans and trousers, outlandish flowered shirts and ties, mini dresses, maxi dresses and all lengths in between, in all the colours of the rainbow with gladiator boots, platform shoes and floppy hats and feather boas.

Music played loudly from open shop doorways as excited shoppers streamed in and out, laden with carrier bags displaying the name of the shop. Attitude, London Girl, Roxette, Chelsea Girl, Snob.

England swings like a pendulum do, bobbies on bicycles two by two, Westminster Abbey, the Tower and Big Ben . . .

'That's a good tune,' said Martha, humming it to herself, as we went around to the back of Attitude and entered through the staff door. Clattering up the stairs, we walked along a little dim corridor when Martha suddenly stopped me and whispered, 'Hey Esther baby, you be prepared for that Pam to question you about Jude? She'll be wanting to know where he is and . . .' She glanced at my left hand and pulled it forward, raking it with her eyes.

'Martha, what are you doing?'

'Why you not wearing your ring?' she said roughly.

'I don't know. I'm not ready to wear it yet . . .'

'You should be. That Pam, she'll be pea-green with envy.'

Pulling my hand back, I said, 'I don't care what Pam thinks.'

'Humph, you tell her it's in the jewellers for sizing, OK? They know you're engaged, Esther baby. They'll wanna see the ring.'

'How do they know I'm engaged?'

'Don't you know how the grapevine works?' And when I just looked puzzled, 'You're such an innocent. But, hey, that's what I like about you. Remember though, in the jewellers for sizing.'

'OK.' I nodded obediently. 'Where's Jude, then? Away on business?'

She thought for a moment and then, nodding sagely, hissed, 'Yeah . . . away on business.'

After exchanging conspiratorial smiles, we pushed through the door and walked straight into the lion's den.

14

Dragging a big box from the sitting room to the bedroom, I tore in to it and began pulling out clothes and putting them into piles of skirts, dresses, trousers, jeans, blouses, T-shirts. fetched hangers and began to hang the clothes in the fitted blonde wood wardrobes that lined one whole wall, a total rarity making me feel both upmarket and privileged.

Gone were the great hulking pieces of furniture that took up so much space. I had a posh, slimline bedroom now.

Going into the kitchen I fetched the little radio and my rapidly cooling coffee and took both into the bedroom. The Beatles blared out from the radio, with just a hint of static so I had to adjust the aerial. *Listen, do you want to know a secret? Do you promise not to tell? Woah, oh oh . . .*

Jigging from one foot to the other, I sipped my coffee, grimacing because it was almost cold. Yuck!

Closer, let me whisper in your ear, say the words you long to hear, I'm in love with you . . .

My mind went back to yesterday when Martha and I had gone into Attitude. We'd gone straight into the changing rooms where Jane and Julie were making up their faces in front of fancy new mirrors. Mrs Rodgers, just coming in from the front of the shop saw me straight away,

'Wow, Esther . . . and Martha too. Good to see you both.'

Faint music could be heard from the shop. *I'm telling you now, I'm telling you right away . . .*

Her legs looked very long and very straight beneath her very short skirt,as if she was walking on stilts. She wore thick, pale blue eye-shadow and pale lipstick. Large white plastic circles swung from her ears. Jane and Julie rushed over enveloping me and Martha in hugs, smelling of some sweet perfume and powder, saying how much they'd missed us and asking if we were coming back.

'Oh,you gotta come back,' implored Julie. 'It's not the same here at Attitude without you two.'

'Well . . .' I looked questioningly at Mrs Rodgers, 'Ah, you know me well enough, Esther baby, I'd bite your hand off.' She pretended to be a dog and went for my hands woofing and growling.

I'll be saying for many a day, I'm in love with you now . . .

Laughing and pulling my hands away, I said, 'I thought you might have replaced me by now.'

'Hey, you're irreplaceable, doll, you know that.'

'Oh yeah, irreplaceable Esther baby,' said a voice and we all looked around to see Pam. She'd been modelling in the shop and wore the most beautiful deep blue evening dress with gloves to the elbow that set off her red hair and cat-green eyes against her flawless white skin.

Why she had such a deep hatred for me and my looks when she looked so good herself, I had no idea.

'What's happened to Sugar Daddy then, huh?' I saw her eyes skitter to my left hand and the curl of her lip when she saw it was empty of rings.

'If you mean Jude,' I said, 'he's away on business at the moment.'

Even though her face was set like stone, her lips gave a little smile as she moved over to a changing room and swished the blood-red curtains across.

'Your engagement ring *away on business at the moment* too?'

All eyes were focussed on me as I said, 'Oh, that . . .' Martha gave me a nudge. 'The ring's in the jewellers being re-sized. It's a tiny bit too big.'

Pam came out of the changing room wearing a robe. Tying it tight at the waist, she sat down in front of a mirror, lit a cigarette and with it dangling between her lips, began to cream her face.

I gave a slight cough before Martha butted in with, 'Yeah, and you know what a ring's like when it's too big, just keeps moving around and around on your finger. Really annoying.' She gave Pam a penetrating black stare.

'When are you wanting to come back, Esther? And you too, Martha?' asked Mrs Rodgers over-cheerfully as if making up for Pam's rudeness.

'Monday?' I asked.

'You're on!' She held out a hand and we shook hard.

Jane, dressed in a beautiful long crocheted dress and a floppy hat, all ready for the catwalk, said, 'I gotta go now Esther, but how's your new flat? Is it as swish as everybody says it is? Fitted wardrobes and all?'

'Yeah . . . I got fitted wardrobes and even a telephone!'

'Wow! Your very own telephone?'

Pam, still busy creaming her face, the cigarette burning in an ash tray now, said sarcastically, 'Next you'll be saying you got one of those brand new trim phones, eh?' And then just loud enough so we could hear, 'And all on the back of a man!'

Martha looked ready to explode, her

face red and taut as a beef tomato, so I said we'd better go and we'd be back Monday. Julie followed us out, and I filled her in on all that had happened with Dennis Simpson since last time I'd seen her.

'Wow,' she said. 'What a complicated story. I'm not sure where I fit in though — are you?'

'You were just unfortunate enough to know me, Julie,' I said.

'Nothing unfortunate about that,' she reassured me. 'At least that weirdo's not your brother, though. He seriously creeped me out when I was holed up in that room surrounded by pictures of you . . . and him talking about you all the time…'

'Oh, Julie…'

'Hey, it's not your fault, Esther, and something good came from it, you've gained a sister,' she said brightly. 'When are you gonna bring her in? We'd love to meet her.'

'Yeah, maybe one day when Pam's not around.'

'Hmm,' said Martha ominously. 'That Pam's a dark soul!'

'Yeah, she's embittered all right,' agreed Julie. 'She's always harping on about being a feminist and doing everything on her own, but what she really wants is a man. Her jealousy's deepened since you took up with Jude.'

'But she's so good to look at herself,' I said. 'She could have anyone.'

'Yeah, but after a while, that black soul will come through,' said Martha. 'You mark my words.' She lowered her head like an angry bull.

'Yeah . . . her dad's a prison officer, so what do you expect?' said Julie carelessly.

'Really?' I asked, a dart of shock going through me, 'A prison officer?'

'Yeah, he saw Dennis Simpson brought in. Pam told me all about it, said she wanted to set my mind at rest.'

'Why didn't you tell me this before?'

She shrugged. 'I didn't think it had anything to do with what happened.'

'Does Pam actually know Dennis

Simpson?'

'Yeah, from Milly's.'

'Oh! The night we went there, I thought that was her first time?'

'Oh no, she was a real regular there . . .'

The radio brought me back to the present, standing alone in the bedroom of my flat.

I'm so tired, tired of waiting, tired of waiting for you . . .

A sudden burning longing for Jude overcame me. I sank down onto the bed, scattering my clothes onto the floor and almost spilling coffee everywhere.

I was a lonely soul, I had nobody til I met you, but you keep-a me waiting . . .

Tears tracking down my cheeks, I put the cup on the bedside cabinet and put my head in my hands.

'Yeah,' I said to the radio. 'Maybe I'm tired of waiting too! I want him here now, Decree Absolute or not, I don't care . . .'

'Weakling,' I chided myself as I pulled myself to my feet. Putting the evil Pam out of my mind, I began again on the arduous task of sorting through all my clothes.

I was making good progress when the phone rang. Still not used to that great black thing and its shrill incessant ring, I stared at it for a second or two, before cautiously picking up the receiver and saying, 'Hello?'

There was a lot of whirring and clicking on the line and then a clipped female voice said, 'Will you accept a long distance call from telephone number 012 66900?'

'Yes,' I stammered, my hand shaking and clutching the receiver hard, knowing it couldn't be anyone but Jude on the line. I had an overwhelming urge to hear him and feel the vibrations of his sexy voice that I knew would make the hairs stand up on the back of my neck.

More whirring and clicking before Jude's voice came on the line, so loud and clear that he could have been standing right next to me — and, oh how I wished he was.

'Esther? Esther baby, it's me, Jude . . .'

'Jude, oh my God, is it really you?'
'Yeah, it sure is. You OK, baby?'
'Yeah . . . I miss you though.'
'Boy, am I glad that you miss me. I wasn't sure you would after last time I saw you.'
'Yeah well . . . I do, Jude . . . really, I do.'
'I miss you too . . . Look, I'm sorry about Dennis Simpson, but I had to tell the police. He had to be put away, again!'
'I know. Did you see him, though? All dressed up in a red wig this time!'
The line crackled so I couldn't hear what he said.
'Have you found her . . . Myra, I mean?' I asked.
'Yeah, I tracked her down . . . and guess what, she's married again. Not the guy she moved out there with, but somebody else. He's massive, must be six foot four and broad too. Reminds me of Marty Valesko.'
'Really? But how did she get married without the Decree Absolute?'
'Beats me, but it was a stupid thing to

do. It's made her a bigamist! You should have seen her face when she saw me. Oh, Esther, I wish I'd had my camera.' He chuckled heartily and continued.

'Don't know if she had to confess to the big guy after my visit. It's been a hard job tracking her down, though, with the change of name and all.'

'What happens next?'

There was a screeching on the line so I had to hold the receiver away from my ear, and then I heard him again.

'You wearing your ring, Esther?'

Gazing down at my bare finger I said without a pang of remorse, 'Yes, of course I am.'

'Oh, I'm glad about that. I thought you meant it when . . . well, you know. Hey, take this number . . . it's my hotel room. Quick, before the line disappears again.'

'OK, I'm ready.'

'012 66900 . . . you got that?'

'Yeah, I got it.'

'Hey tell Martha to get her best hat out 'cos those wedding bells will soon be ringing.'

'What about me? Do I have to get my best hat ready?'

'You need to get your best dress ready, baby, something lacy and clingy.'

'Oh, Jude . . .'

'Has Buddy been in touch?'

'No, but Jude . . . I've gone back to Attitude . . .'

There was no reply, then a long shrill beep like a flat line. Then, 'Esther . . . I . . . love...'

The line became crackly and his words indistinct, but I held the receiver to my ear saying, 'Jude? Jude?'

The line was dead and he was gone, but I had a number for him; I knew that he'd be back with the Decree Absolute and that some day soon he'd be mine.

Slipping my hand into the top drawer of the bedside cabinet, I found the envelope containing the key to the PO Box and my engagement ring.

Without hesitation this time and because it felt so right, I slipped it on my finger.

* * *

'Hey Esther, come and have a look at this,' whispered Julie who, holding a local newspaper, beckoned me with a nod of her head. Pam and Jane were modelling in the shop with Mrs Rodgers looking on, so we were alone. Martha was here too but, hey, I have no secrets from her.

Julie spread out the newspaper and pointed with a long red nail to an article featured prominently on the second page with the headline, *Local Barman Court Date Set*.

I got closer to the paper so I could read it, Martha peering over my shoulder.

Local man Dennis Simpson, a barman in Milly's night club in Soho, has been set a court date for the kidnapping of Julie Foster, a model in Attitude clothes shop and the attempted kidnap and stalking of Esther Chambers, former model in Attitude but now personal assistant to Private Investigator, Jude Dunbar.

In their capacity as Private Investigator

and Assistant, Mr Dunbar and Ms Chambers rescued Julie Foster from 10 Norfolk Terrace where she had been imprisoned for almost two weeks. Dennis Simpson, formerly known as Dennis Fishbourne, was a stolen baby, abducted from his pram shortly after his birth in 1924. The court date has been set for September 17.

Julie, Martha and I stared at each other, mouths agape.

'Oh my,' I said. 'So much information in so few words.'

'The court date is so far away,' complained Julie.

'Hmm, these things take time,' explained Martha. 'There's a lot to organise for a court hearing, Julie.'

'Yeah but three months . . . come on!'

'Reporters!' I said. 'They get to know everything, don't they? They even know all about Dennis being an abducted baby!'

'Yeah, well, it was front page news in its day,' said Martha. 'It might seem a long time ago to you two with your youthful faces. But for an oldie like me, the newspaper hasn't been used to wrap my fish and chips yet . . . know what I mean?'

'Yeah, I get what you mean, Martha, but they didn't really have to mention it, did they?'

'Sensationalism,' she said. 'That's what newspapers create, it's what they like. People buy papers if there's a great big glaring headline. A sensational headline . . .'

'Hey, what's going on here, Women's Institute or something?'

We all three turned around to see Mrs Rodgers, hands on her hips, a glare on her face.

'Sorry Mrs Rodgers,' I said, 'We were just looking at the paper. Here, read this.'

'Hmm,' she grunted, snatching the paper away and bringing it close to her face. I swear she's short-sighted but too vain to wear glasses. 'Wow . . . well, that's good. I hope he suffers for what he put you and Julie through and gets a good long sentence. I really do . . . but at the same time I'm paying you to work, not stand around having *Story Time With Mother*!'

'OK, you've made it clear, Mrs Rodgers,' said Martha, her pudgy hands firmly on her hips. 'Are there customers out there waiting?'

'Well,' Mrs Rodgers swallowed. 'Not at this exact moment but there will be soon, so get ready!'

Pam and Jane came back from the shop floor, both of them glowing from the hot lights in the shop, although Pam looked a bit more strung out and heady than usual. She said to Mrs Rodgers, 'There are some people waiting out there now . . . somebody asking for Esther baby, you better tell Martha to go pick up her outfits.'

Mrs Rodgers shook her head, her mouth set as Pam sashayed past and went straight into what she'd claimed as her changing room, swishing the curtains back with a flourish. I was really surprised that Mrs Rodgers hadn't told her in no uncertain terms to tell us herself.

'She's got a date with some guy out there,' mouthed Jane to Julie. I watched the two of them close together, whispering, but knew I would find out later from Julie what had happened. I had more pressing things to do, now that I'd been asked for by name. Martha, walking just ahead of me, swished open the blood red curtain of the changing room, dresses, coats, and skirts, hung over her arm like the drooping neck of a swan.

'Come on, Esther baby, you and these outfits are gonna create a storm!'

'That's more like it, Martha,' said Mrs Rodgers, clapping her hands. 'Chop chop.'

15

With a click, the lid of the case sprang open. It took a moment or two for it to register and, even then, knowing it was empty, my hands still automatically searched the slippery material of the interior expecting to find all those crisp notes that I'd stacked up in there not so long ago.

I'd taken it from the PO Box myself so knew the cases had been switched . . . but how? How? I went into the kitchen and made coffee, hot and fragrant, which I sipped as I walked backwards and forwards across the sitting room floor, my mind whirring with every possibility.

Julie word's stuck in my mind. *Pam's dad's a prison officer. He saw Dennis Simpson brought in*. Is that how Dennis Simpson escaped?

The glimpse of red hair when I left the case in the phone box . . . I'd assumed Dennis Simpson had been standing behind me wearing a wig, but it could have been somebody with red hair.

Pam! She took the case from the phone box and replaced it with this empty one. Dennis Simpson, wearing a red wig, picked up the empty one and got nabbed by the police — but what does it matter? Pam's dad will get him out!

Pam . . . the only red-headed person I knew. Could she be mixed up in this? Had she been working with Dennis Simpson all along? Was I being fanciful or could this really happen? All I could think with my private eye brain, was *yes, it could happen*!

The case with the money could be in Attitude in Pam's dressing room — the dressing room she'd so recently claimed as her own. No one ever did that before, we'd always used whichever changing room was free.

Pam! My thoughts kept going back to her. Did she have the case with the money? If she did, she certainly hadn't planned on me going back to work at Attitude and finding out her little secret.

I didn't mind the money going to Dennis Simpson, but to Pam? No!

Jude. I had to speak to Jude. I went to the bedroom and, sitting on the bed, dialled his room in the hotel. It rang on and on.

Come on Jude, pick up . . .

No reply. Where was he? At this time of day, so early, shouldn't he be in his room?

I knew I'd have to go to Attitude. Somehow, I had to search Pam's changing room. I'd feel better if Jude was with me, but by then it could be too late. Pam might take off with this guy Jane and Julie had been gossiping about, and take the money with her.

I tried Jude's number again. It rang and rang and then there was a whirr and a click and a voice said, 'Hollywood Hotel, how may I help you?'

Taken off guard, I stammered, 'Hello? Could I speak to Mr Jude Dunbar, please? I've rung his room but there's no answer.'

'Ah . . .please hold a moment,

madam.' There were more whirrs and clicks and then the voice again. 'According to our records, Mr Jude Dunbar checked out last night, madam.'

'Oh . . . OK, thank you.'

I hung up, wondering what was going on. Was he on his way back here? If he was, why hadn't he rung to let me know?

Shrugging on my trench coat and belting it tight at the waist, I glanced in the mirror as I tied a chiffon scarf over my hair. Picking up the case, I left the flat and went down the stairs, my knee-high boots tip tapping on every step. Pushing through the door, I went out into the fresh air.

It was a dull day, the sky covered by grey gold-tinged clouds and spots of rain spat onto the pavement. There was a chilly breeze. Martha and I weren't due in at work today, so I would have to bluff my way through this somehow.

I hurried along the busy streets, the case feeling heavy and cumbersome as I walked. My heart thumped and my stomach churned. Oh, how I wished

Jude was here.

The usual crowds had gathered on Carnaby Street, all the young people preening like peacocks in their colourful outfits.

Just as I was about to go around to the back door of Attitude, I heard a voice calling.

'Hey, Esther baby, wait up . . .'

I stopped in the middle of the path, my heart thumping harder than ever. I spun round, not believing it, but knowing it had to be true. I'd recognise that voice anywhere.

'Jude!'

He held out his arms and I ran straight into their safe curve, dropping the case, as I squeezed tightly into him.

'Oh, Esther baby, Esther baby,' he crooned, as he lifted me off my feet, spinning me round and round, until he set me down and our mouths met in a tingling explosion. People smiled and stared as they walked past.

'Come on,' he said. 'Let's go for a coffee. We need to talk before we do anything rash.'

Arm in arm we went to the nearest café and, finding a seat in the busy place, Jude ordered drinks for both of us. Glancing at him I saw that he looked tired. He was unshaven and stubbly, dark circles beneath his eyes, but they still shone and sparkled as blue as a summer sky.

'I can't believe it,' I said, touching his arm, the material of his coat soft beneath my fingers. 'I was wishing for you, and now you're here.'

He gave a sexy grin and said, 'Look.' He took a paper from his breast pocket and placed it in front of me on the yellow Formica-topped table. 'I got it. It took some doing, but I got it . . . now we can set a date!'

Almost reverently I touched the Decree Absolute before asking, 'What's happened to Myra?'

The waitress came with the coffees which she set on the table with a clatter. Jude grinned as he pushed his hat to the back of his head and took a sip of the hot, dark liquid.

'She has a five-thousand-dollar fine and her marriage to the big guy is null and void.'

'Wow,' I said. 'So what's she gonna do?'

'She wants to marry again but the big guy is in two minds now.'

He shrugged as I said, 'Why?'

'Because she lied to him. She's paying with her happy marriage for not lodging the Decree Absolute in the first place.'

Fumbling in his pocket, he took out a pack of cigarettes and lighting up, took a deep drag.

'How come you're here, though, Jude? How did you know I'd be going to Attitude today? Why didn't you ring before you left? There's so much to explain. Tell me . . .' I picked up my cup, cradling it in both hands as I took a sip.

He took another drag on the cigarette, turning his head as he blew out a long funnel of grey smoke.

'It was the early hours when I left, I didn't want to wake you. You mentioned that you'd gone back to Attitude, so I thought I'd try there before going to your flat. I got a night flight, dropped my bag at my place and then came here. I'd got what I went across the pond for and I had a hunch when you mentioned red hair. I got an instant picture of the model who seems to dislike you so much.'

'Yeah,' I butted in. 'Pam . . .'

The people at the table next to ours stood up to leave, their chair legs scraping on the floor, making me cringe. I could hear a record playing. *Going to the movies only makes me sad, parties make me feel as bad . . .*

'Jude . . . her dad's a prison officer, I think he helped Dennis Simpson escape . . . and I think . . .'

'Pam has the case containing the money?'

'Yes!'

When I'm not with you, I just don't know what to do . . .

'That case felt heavy when I put it in the PO Box, Esther.' He stubbed out the cigarette in a small tin ash tray. 'I'd bet my bottom dollar it contained money then.'

'You mean, it could have been swapped after putting it in the PO Box, not before?'

I drained my coffee and put the cup back into the saucer with a click.

'There's the possibility of either way. Pam's dad could have swopped it from the PO Box.'

Like a summer rose, needs the sun and rain . . .

I told him about Pam taking a changing room as her very own whereas, before I'd gone back to Attitude, we'd used whichever was free.

'I need to look in that changing room, Jude, right now. Come on . . .'

Decisively I stood up, picking up the case. Jude stood up too and together we left the café and walked outside. Soft rain hung in the air in silver sheets that caressed the ground light as a feather as we made our way to Attitude.

* * *

We went in through the back door and, once in the corridor, Jude pulled me back and said, 'Leave the case here with me. Go in and find an excuse for looking in that changing room. OK?'

I nodded and went through into the changing area. To my surprise there was no one there. I'd been prepared for questions from Mrs Rodgers and Jane and Julie, black looks from Pam, wanting to know why I was there. *Hey, coming in on your day off . . . what's going on, Esther baby*?

Sidling into the changing room Pam had taken over, I raked it over with my eyes before peering behind the curtain, putting my hand down behind the little wooden seat, looking beneath the clothes she'd allowed to pile up on the floor.

I caught sight of myself in the full length mirror, a skinny young woman, my waist the span of two hands, yet my face and my eyes 'breathtakingly beautiful' as Jude was so fond of saying. Shaking my head, yet secretly pleased at Jude's comments, I turned away, gazing around the room again, wondering where she'd hidden the case.

There was nowhere else to look, it being only a small area. Yet, going back to the mirror, I noticed that something didn't sit right with it — it looked as if it had been moved forward from the wall. Squeezing my hand into the little space behind, I was surprised to find my hand flailing about in a hole. Stretching even further back, my arm up to the elbow disappearing, I felt something square and hard. I pulled again at the mirror but couldn't budge it. I'd have to fetch Jude.

Going to the door to the corridor, I cracked it open a tiny bit and whispered, 'Jude, I need your help.'

Holding a finger to my lips, he followed me as we crept back into Pam's changing room where I pointed out the mirror, whispering, 'There's something behind there.'

Then I heard a voice.

'Hey, what's going on?'

I peered out from between the curtains.

'Mrs Rodgers, it's only me, Esther . . .'
'What you doing here, Esther baby? Miss the place so much, you have to come in on your day off?'
I giggled and said, 'I've lost an earring and thought it might be here somewhere.'
Jude, breathing heavily, whispered 'Damn' as he tried to get his hand into the narrow space between the mirror and the wall.
'Well,' she said, standing straight and tall, showing all her long legs, her arms crossed over her breasts. 'That's Pam's dressing room, she'll go crazy if she sees you in there. She'll be out any time now.'
'A dressing room's a dressing room,' I said. 'How come Pam has her own now?'
Jane and Julie came up behind Mrs Rodgers, Julie giving me a penetrating gaze as if she knew everything that was going on.
'You OK, Esther?' she asked.
'Yes, of course,' I assured her.
'You know how Pam is,' explained Mrs Rodgers. 'Likes to keep things to

herself.'

'Yeah, well,' I replied, 'It's a mess in here, all the clothes over the floor. She sure needs someone to look after her.'

Behind me I heard Jude grunt as he pulled harder and harder at the mirror, after which there was a dragging sound, and then a satisfying click.

Quietly, he said, 'Yep, the money's here, Esther . . . you can come clean now.'

I pulled back the curtain with a flourish to reveal Jude, the open case full of money beside him, the mirror pulled away to reveal a deep hole in the wall.

Mrs Rodgers gave a groan and put her hands to her mouth. Jane and Julie gaped wide-eyed as Pam sashayed into the room dressed up to the nines, a beautiful black gown clinging to her curves.

Her face was haughty and oblivious at first and then, more and more white and taut, as the reality of the whole situation began to dawn on her — and on me too.

With a sick feeling in the pit of my stomach, I realised she'd been working with Dennis Simpson all along — even with the kidnapping of Julie.

She stood still, her hands on her hips, and gave a deep throaty laugh.

'Well, well, Esther baby, super sleuth!' She laughed so hard, bending slightly holding her stomach, that tears came into her eyes and ran unheeded down her cheeks.

Jude was speaking into his walkie talkie to the police. Music echoed from the front of the shop.

Please lock me away, and don't allow the day, here inside, where I hide with my loneliness . . .

'Oh for God's sake,' said Mrs Rodgers, the tips of her fingers to her forehead. 'Not the police again! Tell them to come round the back of the shop, and tone it down with the siren and the blue light!' Glaring at Pam, she said, 'What on earth have you done?'

'You won't be taking off with your sugar daddy and all Esther's money now, will you, Pam?' said Julie.

So I wait and in a while, I will see my true love smile, she may come, I know not when . . .

Jane scurried away as Mrs Rodgers instructed her to go and lock the front doors of the shop and pull down the blinds. 'I don't want no more customers coming in today.' She looked close to tears.

I don't care what they say, I won't stay in a world without love . . .

'Oh, Pam,' moaned Mrs Rodgers again. 'What have you done?'

16

The chapel was cool and dim, a wonderful escape from the unexpected heat of an Indian summer. Dust motes like tiny fairies floated in shimmering bands of sunlight that fell through the beautiful stained glass windows set deep into the chapel's thick walls.

Jesus hung limply from the cross as angels heralded him, haloes adorning their foreheads like bright bands of gold. There was an odour of damp and incense and the slow, steady burning of wax candles that flickered on the deep window sills.

I stood quietly alone, breathing deeply, my hands, the fingers entwined, resting on the creamy richness of my wedding gown. My gown that fitted tightly across my breasts, with a high neck and long, lacy sleeves that finished in a point at my middle finger, and that puffed out from the waist, as if a hoop was underneath, like Scarlett O'Hara's dress fashioned out of curtains that she hoped would cajole Rhett into giving her money.

Closing my eyes, I thought of everything that had happened over the past few turbulent months in which so much has been revealed about my past, such long-hidden secrets about my parentage. Things I'd never have found out without the help of Jude and Suzanne — oh, and Marty Valesko and Dennis Simpson too, in a way.

Without Jude I wouldn't have been lucky enough to become a private investigator, and learn that one of the most important things about the job is to always wear two pairs of tights underneath your mini-skirt otherwise you'll soon freeze to death!

I heard a noise behind me and a voice.

'Hey, here you are, Esther baby . . . and oh my, you look more like Grace Kelly than she ever does herself!'

Glancing around, I did a double take at Martha all dressed up in her wedding finery.

'Oh Martha! You look fabulous . . . and that hat is the best!'

'Yeah well, Jude said I was to get out my best hat when wedding bells rang, and I ain't gonna disappoint him.'

I laughed as she said, 'Pretty enough for you, Esther baby?' as she did a twirl, her baby blue gown, exactly the same as Suzanne's, swinging around her. 'Heck, I don't know about being a dresser, Mrs Rodgers will want me as a model when she sees me today.'

She went back to the door and, cracking it open a little, shouted through, 'Come on, Suzanne . . . your sister's in here, she's been hiding herself away all along.'

'There are hordes of people coming into the church,' said Suzanne with excitement, and then on seeing me, she took my hands and said, 'You look so beautiful, Esther . . .'

'So there should be a lot of people,' said Martha with an emphatic nod. 'Esther baby's gonna be Queen for the day.'

'Well,' I said, gathering Suzanne and Martha in close to me, 'I might not have a dad to walk me down the aisle, but I've certainly got a lovely new sister and one of the best friends I've ever had, who, I'm sure will do the job just as well.'

'Oh no don't, Esther baby,' said Martha, as she fumbled in the pocket of her dress for a tissue. 'You'll be bringing on the tears and I don't want to spoil my make-up, not at this late stage of the game.'

I gave them both a small posy of flowers and, clasping my own, the strains of the Wedding March suddenly struck up.

Martha said softly, 'We pray for a glorious wedding that the bride and groom will cherish for a lifetime.'

With those words giving me courage, I took a deep breath. As the great heavy oak doors opened, I pulled my beautiful embroidered veil over my face and, just as countless brides had done before me, took the long walk down the aisle, Suzanne and Martha following closely behind.

The church was as packed as Suzanne had said it would be, with so many familiar faces. I could see Julie and Jane, with Mrs Rodgers holding a bunched up tissue to her face; Marty Valesko, giving a slight bow as I floated by; and Tony with Marie at his side. I recognised customers from Attitude and family from Jude's side, including all the Ms the'd told me so much about — Maud, Marilyn, Milly and Miranda. I mourned the loss of my mum and dad, wishing they could have been with me on such a happy day, as, finally, I arrived at the altar and Martha and Suzanne backed away and left me alone with Jude.

* * *

I'm in the mood for love, simply because you're near me, I'm in the mood for love . . . Jude hummed the rest of the tune and pulled me in tight for the bridal dance at our wedding reception. Everyone watched us as we moved around the dance floor gazing into each other's eyes.

My stomach somersaulted at the twinkle in his baby blues.

'You sang this song to me first time you asked me to marry you,' I whispered in his ear. 'And the same day I found out about Dennis Simpson having been stolen away from my parents.'

'Oh yes, I remember that,' Jude whispered back, 'We were in the library...'

'You remember?' I said, pretending to be shocked.

'Yeah, sure I do . . . hard not to when you turned me down! Worst day of my life!'

I giggled and he said, 'You see, we've made memories already and we've only just got married.'

Funny but when you're near me, I'm in the mood for love, Heaven is in your eyes, bright as the stars we're under . . .

A few other couples got up too and started dancing around us. Marty Valesko was with a pretty woman wearing a short dress and platform boots, Suzanne and a young man with floppy blond hair, and Martha with her husband, George, who got a double take from Jude when he saw her fancy hat. Even Tony and Marie swayed together, caught up tight in a lover's clinch.

Suddenly I caught a flash of red from the corner of my eye and looked around so quickly, I almost got whiplash.

'Hey,' said Jude, glancing at me and grinning, 'Don't get spooked, Esther baby, it's not her...'

'What do you mean?' I said quickly.

Oh, is it any wonder, I'm in the mood for love . . .

'It's not Pam . . . she's gone now. You don't have to worry about her any more . . . nor Dennis Simpson . . . nor even Pam's dad, the prison officer.'

'Well, somebody's got red hair, Jude — so who is it?'

If there's a cloud above, if it should rain we'll let it . . .

'It's Buddy's wife, Cheryl, look . . .'

We danced past and waved at them, Buddy and his wife, a tall, bony woman with curly red hair, enthusiastically they waved back.